Praise for
WEDDING AT THE GRAVEYARD

"Rabbi Nilton Bonder summarizes his view on the paranormal with the old Castilian expression, 'I don't believe in brujas [witches], but they are there, they are.'"

—PEDRO ARBEX, *Brazil Journal*

"There are those who claim to see dead people, those who claim to speak to the afterlife, those who claim to have access to memories of supposed past lives, and even those who swear to be able to move objects with the power of their mind. Charlatans aside, a portion of the phenomena still remains without an explanation that is independent of some level of faith. And it was in this territory of the incredible-fantastic-extraordinary that Rabbi Nilton Bonder focused on telling the stories of his 29th book."

—RONALD VILLARDO, *O Globo*

"With charm, precision, and humor, *Wedding at the Graveyard* offers a fascinating perspective on unexpected events—many of which blur the line between real and fantastical—that have shaped Rabbi Nilton Bonder's worldview. Original and thought-provoking, Bonder's prose sparkles with insight and surprise."

—GEORGIA HUNTER, *New York Times* bestselling author of *We Were the Lucky Ones*

"Drawing on his extensive experience as a student of Jewish wisdom and his role as a spiritual teacher and counselor, Rabbi Nilton Bonder shares his encounters with the mysterious and inexplicable—events that defy logic, embrace paradox, and challenge our understanding of what's possible. The fascinating and often humorous stories he shares invite us to consider that reality extends beyond what meets the eye, and suggest there is a hidden dimension. Through our encounters with these mysteries, we can open doors to greater spiritual awareness and discover a richer, deeper experience of life itself."

—RABBI J. ROLANDO MATALON, B'nai Jeshurun, New York City

WEDDING AT THE GRAVEYARD

AND OTHER TALES OF THE JEWISH FANTASTICAL

NILTON BONDER

Paperback ISBN 978-1-958972-68-7
eBook ISBN 978-1-958972-69-4

Library of Congress Cataloging-in-Publication Data

Names: Bonder, Nilton, author.
Title: Wedding at the graveyard : and other tales of the Jewish fantastical / Nilton Bonder.
Description: Rhinebeck, New York : Monkfish Book Publishing Company, 2025.
Identifiers: LCCN 2024056237 (print) | LCCN 2024056238 (ebook) | ISBN 9781958972687 (paperback) | ISBN 9781958972694 (eBook)
Subjects: LCSH: Parapsychology--Religious aspects--Judaism. | Extrasensory perception.
Classification: LCC BM538.P2 B66 2025 (print) | LCC BM538.P2 (ebook) | DDC 296.3/71--dc23/eng/20241206
LC record available at https://lccn.loc.gov/2024056237
LC ebook record available at https://lccn.loc.gov/2024056238

Book and cover design by Colin Rolfe

Monkfish Book Publishing Company
22 East Market Street, Suite 304
Rhinebeck, New York 12572
(845) 876-4861
monkfishpublishing.com

CONTENTS

THE STORIES

AUTHOR'S NOTE

All the stories narrated here are true. By true, I mean that these events actually occurred. The big question is, where exactly did these events take place? I recount events spanning nearly four decades, during which I encountered the allegories of mysticism and the spiritual realm. Indeed, religion and beliefs, a realm of metaphors and existential insinuations, leave no one untouched.

What are faith and its doctrines if not the manifestation of ghosts, auras, and souls that human beings perceive in their bodies? The psychic experience sees in itself something of the parapsychic order. How could it be otherwise? Self-consciousness is a ghost that inhabits us as an effect of thought, which, in turn, is aware of itself. Thus, a parallel entity haunts us. This character is nothing more than the "I"—a subject who, within us, lives around these twilight zones—the liminal places we inhabit, the thresholds of our everyday lives.

Was it, or wasn't it? Did it happen, or did it not happen? Was I awake, or was it a dream? What's the guarantee that my experience was not a dream or a delirium? And it is precisely because of the lack of any witness other than oneself that we often live in a state close to dreaming.

This realm, akin to a trancelike state, encompasses experiences we observe with deep skepticism. This is not the suspicion of an act of deliberate fraud, but the recognition that, in addition to factual reality, psychic activity produces another reality as well. And when two realities coexist, that liminal zone emerges, capable of both confirmation and contestation with the same conviction. Passing through this zone produces sounds, visions, and perceptions that, strange and distorted, appear to be from another world. Or the other world. Or this world. Which is it, and where are we?

The intersection of reality and reality generates effects and soundtracks that define the mysteries. Each mystery's theme is that it transitions from normal time to a state of slow motion and distorted sound, a phenomenon that arises from the coexistence of two realities. Validating one over the other seems unnecessary, like saying one is true and the other false. This would only produce delirium or sanity, not two realities.

In general terms, the experiences described in these stories are not madness, hallucinations, or dementia. However, neither are they factual or substantiated. They are intersections between internal and external reality, indisputable creations, and truthful versions. Their nature is both improbable—not verifiable in the laboratory—and absolutely proven by indisputable personal experience.

If you don't feel fear or vertigo when in contact with liminality, then join me in my storytelling. This is why "history" and "story" are factual and fictional, respectively. By definition, the two realities never intersect; they merely draw near each other, and it is this phenomenon of approximation between realities that the liminal space embodies.

These are stories derived from my forty years as a rabbi, in which I witnessed colliding realities. When these collisions take place, they often release a significant amount of light and energy, akin to a sudden burst that, rather than settling or defining, opens up both possibilities, leading to a sense of disruption in consciousness. Therefore, it is because of these cracks and crevices—as the poet Leonard Cohen said—that the most penetrating rays of light escape. So come with me, armed with decisive certainty that all this has really, undoubtedly, happened.

BEYOND IMAGINATION

In black and white, the television program came on with that music, something like that of Hitchcock's *Psycho*, announcing another episode of *Além da imaginação*, "*Beyond Imagination*" in Portuguese. The original title in English was *The Twilight Zone*. I think it was black-and-white television, or the 1960s itself, that set the tone for the series. In that decade of flying saucers, it could have been about Russians or humans traveling to the moon in a possible Yankee (go home!) farce to dominate the world, or hippies and Brazilian tropicalist musicians challenging the status quo of squareness and dictatorship; everything suggested a twilight zone, on the border of uncertainty and suspicion.

I was a boy, and did I know about this! The program aired on Fridays, following *The Munsters*, a satirical series about a supernatural family of frankensteins and vampires.

Despite its comic tone and parody of ogres and abnormalities, there was still something sinister about it. My parents were often out in the evening, so at bedtime I couldn't count on their presence at home. The atmosphere of insecurity created an appropriate climate for the battle between tiredness and sleep, as well as the stubborn resistance to not surrender to either. *The Twilight Zone* would then commence.

Given that it was mandatory, the juvenile court would issue a warning, stating that they purposely aired this program late and approved it for audiences over the age of sixteen, thereby heightening the atmosphere of mystery. It wasn't exactly midnight, but it was late enough to produce a sense of an endless and distorted time in the wait for the parents' return.

On the screen there were "histories," such as... A woman stops a man on the road on a stormy night, pleading for help. When the man exits his car, he notices another vehicle that has crashed into a river, threatening to drown two children, whom he bravely rescues. Soon after, he realizes that the woman who had just called for help was dead in the front seat. Dead or alive? What would be true? Of course, the suggestion was that a mother, desperate to protect her children from danger, would overcome the boundaries between life and death. However, the combination of the maternal issue and the absence of my real parents at home created a unique meaning for me, eliciting an involuntary gesture of agreement, as if to affirm, "Yes, that is quite possible, though unlikely!"

I think television back then, with its limited special effects, was more captivating than today. Technology has taken away that homely, crafty feel, much more conducive to producing the creepy and horrifying than today's computerized resources. The early effects were less fake than the hyper-realism of special effects. The unpretentious approach offers a more authentic appearance and feel, effectively capturing the drama that resonates with us. The supernatural aspects of the digital world and artificial intelligence are much less convincing.

It is in keeping with the spirit of this program that I present the following stories. They also follow the fabulous tradition of the rabbis, who told their parables to enter a world of paradoxes. Paradoxes are nothing more than descriptions of the phenomenon of two realities coming too close together. For instance, it is from the rabbinic world that the word "abracadabra" (let what I say take place!) comes; the Golem, precursor to Mary Shelley´s *Frankenstein*; and the friendly Endora, mother of the Enchantress and inspired by the witch Endor, who communicates with the dead at the request of the biblical King Saul.

This is life in its encounter with the unusual and inventive, highly volatile, and combustible chemical of imagination. This is life, in fact, beyond imagination.

THE STORIES

Rabbi Hanina prohibited individuals from sleeping alone in a house
due to the possibility of Lilith capturing them.
When a person is alone, a destructive spirit can harm them.
When two people are present, the spirit can appear but not harm anyone.
With three people present, he doesn't even speak!

TALMUD BER 43B

THE GHOST OF THE RARE MANUSCRIPT ROOM

I did my rabbinical studies at The Jewish Theological Seminary, a community of scholars and students in a classic building typical of aristocratic universities, located in Manhattan, bordered on one side by Columbia University and on the other by Harlem. At first, I lived in the dormitory adjacent to the university building, with its high ceilings and long corridors decorated with paintings of presidents and personalities from the past; most of them had already graduated from this world. It was a place where a painting's eyes seemed to follow us as we strolled down the corridor.

I worked at the library for minimum wage to survive those days. That was when an opportunity arose. The library offered me a job to work with its Iberian Collection of Rare Manuscripts because I am from Latin America and speak Portuguese and Spanish. This would mean doubling my salary, and so I didn't hesitate. I left the modern and luxurious headquarters, and went to work in the tower, where the old library was. The Rare Manuscripts Room, located at the top of the tower with restricted access, housed priceless manuscripts, books, and editions.

It was curious that one of the biggest threats to these manuscripts came from the Orthodox Jewish community. They believed that several sacred documents were in the hands of "infidels" and periodically tore out pages or took fragments from them as a "devotional" act, aimed at preventing them from falling into the hands of liberal, non-Orthodox Jews. They often tried to steal these priceless manuscripts, and sometimes they were caught attempting to do so. It wasn't uncommon to see photos of Orthodox and Hasidic people displayed on posters in New York libraries, showing them as dangerous criminals.

At my new place of work, to enter, you had to go through a steel door, similar to a safe. Surrounded by old books and scrolls, I received a warning that the door would always remain closed for security. I would work alone. I had to use a bell or an intercom to unlock the door when I wanted to leave. They also informed me that there was a sophisticated chemical-based fire system on the premises. In the early 1960s, a devastating fire severely damaged the collection, primarily due to the water used by the firefighters, prompting the installation of a dry chemical-based system. When an emergency arose, the alarm would activate, giving me approximately three minutes to evacuate the room before the highly toxic chemicals began to spray.

The room exuded a certain awe due to its closure and associated risks. As if that weren't enough, its interior was quite distinctive, almost macabre. Arranged on shelves, or occasionally left on tables, the manuscripts carried the weight of time and history as they awaited cataloging.

My job was to register and inventory several lots sold at auctions or acquired via donation and that belonged to the Iberian Collection of the Rare Manuscripts Room. Concerning the library's collection, there was particular interest in writings and manuscripts from the time of the Inquisition on the Iberian Peninsula. From the fourteenth to the sixteenth centuries, there were many Inquisition records—original and authentic documents from the Vatican "Holy Office" with processes against Jews and New Christians—a term used for Sephardic Jews and others who were baptized into the Catholic Church following the Edict of Expulsion in 1492. Many of the acquired documents, still stored in boxes and cabinets, I organized and described.

They then brought many of those manuscripts, some quite rare (for example, a letter from the philosopher Maimonides from the twelfth century), in batches. Acquiring only specific manuscripts of interest was not feasible; one had to purchase them collectively, in lots. These were collections that had belonged to individuals who, after passing away, donated or sold them in a closed package. For this reason, in addition to texts of interest, we received others that had little or nothing to do with the library's specialty. I was responsible for distinguishing valuable texts from the more irrelevant ones.

That's how I began reading and organizing notebooks containing the records of the Inquisition. The documents were highly intriguing primary sources of information. They were typically brief, consisting of no more than two or three lines, presenting the narrative and arguments of accusation against defendants, as well as, on occasion, a sentence that had already passed. They were small spectacles filled with drama and intrigue. Endless lists of cases that sealed people's fates, often depriving them of their possessions and their lives.

Through this voyeurism of intimacy and routine from five or six centuries ago, I learned about the petty feelings that fueled many of these processes. It was not uncommon to find texts that read: "Mr. Such and Such accuses Mr. So and So, who lives on Such and Such Street, of being a Judaizer or of practicing witchcraft." The description of his profession reveals that both the informant and the accused were shoemakers. It was clear that personal interests, fueled by an entire whistleblowing culture, were behind the incriminations.

Alternatively, I would come across articles about a girl who had publicly criticized another girl of the same age. I couldn't help but imagine that the motivation behind this denunciation could be a suitor they were both vying for, or some other unpleasant motive. Who knows! And so I worked, hours on end, immersed in seemingly childish and superfluous plots that had brought a lot of pain and despair to real people.

The past is always ghostly, as we only know a few details from which, through the imagination, we recreate entire and real lives, materializing "flesh and bone" figures through fragments of their suffering. All this filled the pages of the writings and my imagination in the tower. Recovering a dead past proved to be somewhat haunting, like slivers of light penetrating the dark immensity of oblivion.

However, among the Inquisition manuscripts, from time to time, other materials appeared, such as old editions of classics or lesser-known books. Some books were not as rare as they were older, yet they still enjoyed the same noble and magisterial sojourn in the pile before me.

Then a certain book fell into my hands. In fact, at first it was difficult to tell if it was a book, because it was a manuscript, possibly a diary. It did, however, have a very intriguing title: *About That Wanton Woman*. I was immediately interested. A priest had penned it in medieval Portuguese as evidenced by the absence of modern Portuguese letters, expressions reminiscent of archaic Spanish, and the unconventional use of burlesque terms. However, it was the content that was most intriguing.

Supposedly written to defame and dishonor a libertine woman and serve as a warning to anyone with similar licentious inclinations, the text seemed to do the opposite. This cleric was busy describing details that would even vex a reader, like me, on the eve of the twenty-first century. The author meticulously detailed every mistake she had made, seemingly driven by a mission to expose the "devil" in this "hymn" of reserve and modesty. He inadvertently stoked lust in the minds of those who read this falsely pious work.

The perversion captivated me, deserving of a study on the pathologies of repression and sadism. In the detailed description of this woman's indecent and perverse acts, the parish priest closely described, through incriminations and repugnance, his own debauchery. Everything was so graphic, even written in medieval Portuguese! This was how, for me, the past began to gain relief and relevance, from out of the pile of medieval inquisitorial torture came this priest's pornography.

I worked with the priest's text for weeks, imagining I would later photocopy the entire parchment. There were no smartphones yet, and it was not simple to get permission to expose manuscripts, most of which were extremely fragile, to photocopy machines. But I thought this material would be good for a *Playboy*-type magazine because of the content, and how exotic it was to hear everything voiced in fourteenth-century Portuguese.

One winter day, with the Parchment Room nearly freezing due to its marble flooring and walls, I went in to spend more time reading what I began to think of as the "x-parchment" about the infamous "wanton woman." It was on a shelf, just above my head. It was the last folder in the row, tilted and supported by other folders, with a minimum of twenty centimeters between it and a stack of old books.

Without looking, I reached my hand upwards to take the salacious parchment off the shelf, and as soon as I did, I touched against something warm—something that was a living thing, an organic thing. With a glance quicker than my reflex to withdraw my hand, I found myself brushing some viscous green material. Even today, I can access that tactile memory—a mixture of touching and feeling that strange substance.

Like an electric shock, an instant shiver took over my body. Fear and disgust made me jump out of my chair and run towards the locked door. The horror and discomfort were so uncontrollable that I was unable to carry out what I had always imagined I would undertake when faced with a supernatural encounter. In moments of irrational fear, perhaps as a tactic, I thought I could calm down by persuading myself of how incredible it would be to witness and experience the transcendent. I believed that curiosity could instill in me a courage that would surpass fear. But it was nothing like this! Like a cartoon character, I yearned for freedom, trying to escape in order to share that apparition with someone else.

I think a large part of horror is not believing what you are seeing or experiencing. Disbelief in front of what the senses attest is always most disturbing.

In my eagerness to ring the bell, so someone could rescue me, I ended up setting off the fire alarm. I had just added another element of panic to the situation, but this time it was due to a real danger: I had only three minutes to escape!

Three minutes is a long time, as I discovered in terror. The alarm sounded, and the door opened in seconds. I walked through it, already screaming that it was a mistake and pleading for the deactivation of the firefighting system. Could anyone hear me?

Then, upon quick investigation, I found that the alarm did not trigger the system automatically, and I never faced the risk of inhaling toxic gases or particles. Still, when they questioned me later, I hesitated to share the details of what had occurred. Without elaborating on what I was sure I had seen, I simply said I'd been scared because of something moving in the Rare Manuscripts Room.

The security guard entered. I followed him, staring at the shelf where the wanton manuscript was located and where everything had happened. Of course, there was nothing to be seen. The security guard said, "Rats. Rats are all over city! I'll alert maintenance so they can put poison and mousetraps here in the tower."

I left feeling shaken and dazzled. What had it been?

But I kept it a secret because, despite witnessing what I saw, I lacked the means to confirm it for myself. It was truly remarkable, not just for what I could see with my eyes, but for the texture of something I had never touched before.

I wondered, to my disgust, that it might indeed have been a rat. But I couldn't convince myself of this. A phosphorescent green mass was what I saw!

I don't hold any beliefs that could validate this conviction or hypothesis. So I know that the room, its vibrations, and its sense of solitude, all contributed to what happened. I also know that the priest's text, brimming with eroticism and fetish, transcended centuries of silence and invisibility, contributing to its materialization.

The following day, I hurried to finish cataloging the Iberian Collection of Rare Manuscripts at The Jewish Theological Seminary. Because everything was almost finished, I was able to complete the job quickly. But due to the double hourly rate for the special project, and the seduction of that libidinous text, I procrastinated.

Then I happily returned to work in the new aseptic library building. The absence of the past preserved the objective assurance of the present, and human senses. I made significantly less money there, and did infinitely more tedious work, compared to the work in the manuscript room. On several occasions, I considered returning to the Iberian Collection in order to photocopy the priest's manuscript, but then as time passed, and especially after I graduated, I forgot all about it.

It must still be there, waiting for someone to bring to life again the troubled perversions of the depraved lady and her tormented inquisitor. Reliefs and concerns are so typical of the past.

WEDDING AT THE GRAVEYARD

Mrs. Sophie was Romanian and lived in Copacabana. It was not the Copacabana of today, but the cosmopolitan and refined district of the writer Clarice Lispector, the painter Cândido Portinari, and the playwright Nelson Rodrigues.

She always left me embarrassed when we passed each other in the neighborhood. She was a direct woman, and always complimented me on my looks, making references to my youthful appearance. In addition to these awkward comments—enough to embarrass the neophyte rabbi—she would do something even worse: whenever our interaction was about to end, she would open her bag and, after a brief search, take out some dollar bills (which she'd folded) and pass them to me. She did this slyly, as if she were disguising an illicit item. Then she would say, "This is for the kids!"—pushing my hand, anticipating a potential refusal. She would do this as if it were a custom or a tradition.

Meeting a rabbi was once considered a good omen, and in old Europe, this feeling of blessing—at least for the well-educated and prosperous—required the gift of a donation. What bothered me was that I felt like a bribed traffic cop. The source of my discomfort stemmed from the fact that I earned a fixed salary, and the circumstances differed from those in Europe goneby, where the community would directly provide support for the rabbi and his family, making these "voluntary" contributions customary, with dire consequences if one failed to comply.

Nevertheless, the fact that the currency of the donation was always in dollars, worked as a mitigating factor, for it seemed more like a gift than money itself. Had she given me Brazilian cruzeiros, there would have been more conviction in the whispered and hesitant phrases I uttered: “It’s not necessary...”—already taking the money without resistance. The sensation of a profitable chance encounter quickly nullified the frisson of discomfort. And so, we performed this strange behavior such that, when it didn’t occur (which was rare), I found myself uncomfortable due to the simple Pavlovian reaction of expectation.

One morning, I received a phone call from Mrs. Sophie. In a serious tone, she asked me if I would do a wedding. Now, if you ask a carpenter if he would make a piece of furniture, or a tailor if he would make a jacket, it’s a sign of some trouble involved. Generally, these preambles suggested a deviation from the normal, implying a commitment and hinting at an exception. These prologues were frequently followed by requests to participate in a mixed marriage, that is, between a Jew and a non-Jew—something that, as a rabbi, I was not authorized to do. So I was already preparing my refusal when the guilt and incrimination for accepting the tips, which now amounted to additional complicity in the impending act, suddenly entered my thoughts.

To “Would you be willing to officiate at a wedding?” I gave a clear and formal “Yes,” hoping to gain some time before then asking, “What kind of a marriage?”

“It isn’t just any wedding! It’s a marriage between a living bride and a dead groom!” she said with absolute normalcy.

What kind of maneuvers does a human being have to make, when sure of something, he suddenly finds himself forced to give in to surprise and recognize himself as unprepared? I was disconcerted because I could not have imagined such a request coming up on my radar. It certainly seemed macabre, and it was obvious that it was an occasion that would involve marital elements I had never before encountered.

Sophie finally took me out of my thoughts: “I’ll explain. My husband died a few weeks ago. We lived together for forty years, but he never wanted to get married; he argued that it would destroy our relationship, and that's how we stayed. As our forty-first anniversary approached, he surprised me with a gift: a dream trip and the promise that, when we returned, we would finally have our wedding. But he passed away in the middle of our travel. It was quite challenging, yet I can't shake this from my mind, and I believe he won't rest until we find a solution. Don't you agree?"

"What do you mean?" I said, perceiving the invitation as both special and dangerous.

What if this was all a ruse? What if the man didn't want to get married, and the crazy woman was tricking someone from another world? A wedding requires the spouse to say yes and fully declare his consent. There is no contract without a signature, and there is no agreement without, at some point, joining hands or resorting to another form of validation. A marriage is between two people. Can a dead person be considered one of them?

The silence that ensued was, however, affectionate. I realized it was something deeper and involved some form of spiritual care. And then it hit me, that I was about to open the doors to interaction between two worlds. More than that, it would entail both an act of free choice and an act of will, potentially compromising someone who is no longer considered a sovereign and legal entity. There was no guardianship statute for the deceased that I could rely on, just as there is the statute for children and adolescents, who are legal dependents.

I overcame my embarrassment because of the "gifts" she always gave me, and I felt a deep empathy. "Dear Sophie, let me think," I said. "You're asking me about something very unusual. I need to think. Furthermore, I need to consult the tradition and seek advice. Please give me some time, and I will come back to you."

She thanked me repeatedly, asking me to understand the importance and urgency that this all had for her.

I hung up the phone with the urge to tell someone. "You won't believe what just happened to me!" However, the thought quickly shifted to: *This is very serious! What if the last thing a man wanted was to get married? Would this be a crime against individual freedom? Would I be practicing or serving as an accomplice to ideological falsehood? What resources does a dead person have to protect their autonomy?*

Fortunately, I had a master over occult matters. In situations like this, to paraphrase the movie *Ghostbusters*, "Who are you going to call? Reb Zalman!"

Reb Zalman Schachter-Shalomi will be a recurring character in several of these fantastic stories of mine. The founder of a new religious denomination in Judaism, he was an enlightened person, as he always had "one foot here and one foot there."

Reb Zalman received his education in the ultra-Orthodox movement, but the 1960s and its revolutions had a profound impact on him. With one foot in tradition and one in the avant-garde, he admired all religions. He was part of the Hasidic lineage, but could also expertly weave issues of reality and unreality, the natural and the supernatural. There was no doubt: Reb Zalman would advise me.

As I imagined, he expressed no surprise at my question. In fact, he became extremely interested in the case. Then he composed himself, demonstrating how pleased he was to be consulted, and said in a rabbinic and forensic tone, "We have to find some precedent, and we need to create a situation in which the 'groom' does not have to express his intention. In a couple days, I'll bring you some suggestions."

And so it was. Reb Zalman proposed treating marriage as a fait accompli, instead of a deliberative act by the deceased. Jewish law establishes marriage not only through a ceremony but also through the acts of sexual consummation and cohabitation, which also validate the marriage.

Therefore, he suggested treating this wedding as a celebration of something already complete and finished, a formalization of what already existed—without resorting to the role of the groom. Strictly speaking, the groom had already manifested himself by living forty years with his wife, and therefore there was no need for the deceased to reaffirm the vows. This is the nature of a post-mortem marriage.

Moreover, Reb Zalman discovered a precedent in history. Shortly after the Six-Day War between Israel and Arab countries, Israel's chief rabbi made available and performed post-mortem marriages for several women pregnant by soldiers killed in the conflict. So that the offspring would not be born, according to tradition, with the disadvantage and character of illegitimate children, the rabbi then officiated in these collective marriages a posteriori.

Now that we had the legal framework to join legal bodies, both in this world and in another, the only challenge left was how to carry out such a task.

How did all of this happen? First, we scheduled Sophie and her beloved's wedding to take place at the Israelite cemetery in Caju, Rio de Janeiro, on a Tuesday morning. I selected this time to ensure that as few people as possible would witness what I was about to accomplish, understanding that not everyone would have the vision to comprehend those circumstances. We went on that day with a *minyan*—a quorum of ten people that is required for a Jewish marriage. And discreetly, to the astonishment of the few employees who were watching from afar, we unfurled the traditional canopy, the *chupa*, over the bride and the dead man's tomb.

I pronounced in Hebrew some blessings suitable for those who reaffirm vows already taken in the past. In the end, I gave Sophie the chalice to drink from, and the rest I poured onto the groom's tomb. Our ritual concluded with the shattering of the chalice, as is customary at a Jewish wedding, and then we left it there at the grave's foot.

It was a cloudy day, but when it was all done Sophie's heart was at peace. Following that situation-specific liturgy, the participants continued in silence, fully sharing the legitimacy of the ceremony they had participated in. Both worlds—this world and the one to come—seemed appeased at the disentanglement of this unfinished business.

On the way out, Sophie thanked me with a smile and said: "You didn't disappoint me!"

It was not the appropriate place for me to receive a gift for "the children." And in addition to all that intense experience, I also learned that giving gifts may not be a favor, but simply an act of affection.

Oh yes, of course—and in this case, they lived happily ever after!

* * *

Years later, after returning from a trip abroad, I learned that Sophie had passed away. I was not at the *Shiva*, the week of bereavement, to explain to the family that it should not be treated and felt as a week of mourning, but of joy for a so-awaited honeymoon!

Our masters taught six aspects regarding demons: in three, they look like angels, and in three, they look like humans. With the angels, they share: 1) wings; 2) flying from one corner of the world to another; and 3) they are able to hear what happens behind the curtain [of the heavens]. With humans, they share: 1) feeding, 2) procreating, and 3) dying.

TALMUD HAGIGA

KABBALAH FROM TIJUCA

One look can change the shape of reality.

Immersed in the daily routine of shepherding his flock, the biblical Moses gazed at a burning bush that remained unconsumed. His contemplative gaze picked out something from reality that would take him on the journey of journeys.

I was in the precarious teachers' room at the Talmud Torah Secondary School in Tijuca, Rio de Janeiro. I think I was a little like Moses, not knowing what to do with my life. I was studying engineering at PUC, the Catholic University in Rio de Janeiro, but I couldn't see a future much further along the path I was taking. You know that feeling of shepherding that leads nowhere, as if immersed in a mediocre setting, just like in a third-rate theater?

I'd already decided to take an adventure and change careers. I was only a few weeks away from embarking on my journey of journeys, which involved attending a rabbinical school and swapping the solidity of engineering for the unusual symbolic world of the rabbinate. At that point, as a twenty-two-year-old, radically changing careers required a conviction I wasn't sure I possessed.

My neighbor, who, like Moses, had a speech impairment with a nasalized voice, verbalized my parents' ambivalence. Once when my father and I met her on the stairs of the apartment building, she inquired what I was studying. My father jumped and said, "Theology!" His attempt to give academic authority and sobriety to the strangeness of having a son as a rabbi didn't go unnoticed by me. And the neighbor quickly reacted: "Another geologist in the family!" I learned that a nasalized voice can also make a listener nasalized. Or was it just an unconscious form of mine, materializing my father's vexation at my professional choice? Who knows? Life is full of mysteries!

During this transition period, I taught history at the school as a side job to earn a living. One day, during a break in the teachers' room—also known as the library—I noticed an old book tucked away in a cupboard. I got up and went to see what it was. The sheets of material required careful handling due to their extreme dryness. Furthermore, the paper crumbled on the shelf, and tiny fragments disintegrated while sticking to my fingers.

I started leafing through what appeared to be a manuscript. Someone had written it in a language I couldn't identify. It wasn't Hebrew, and it didn't look Arabic to me. I located the desk in the room's corner and inquired with the librarian. "Whose is this?"

"There's only old stuff there," she replied. "When someone passes away, their families dispose of everything in that area. If you want to take anything, you'll do us a favor!"

"Can I really take it?"—I wanted to assure myself.

"Of course, it may all go into the trash," she said in a disinterested tone.

The book had drawings that seemed like Kameoth, an ancient form of amulet common in medieval Kabbalist works. They were magic squares representing the planets, associated with protection and the challenges of destiny. I don't know what moved me to take this book, but the fact is that I put it in a plastic bag to protect the fragments that had come loose and found a place for it in my suitcase, taking it with me when I left for my studies in New York. I packed the so-called amulet book in my luggage, along with a host of other fears about the uncertain future I faced.

It was a hot and humid summer day when I arrived in New York City late at night. I remember there was a garbage worker's strike, and, in addition to the garbage scattered throughout the city, an acidic odor from decomposing waste entered my nostrils. Being alone in Manhattan at the turn of the 1980s was frightening, as the differences between developed countries and Brazil seemed abysmal. Nowadays, everything is very similar everywhere. At that time, people would dream of getting electronic devices not yet available in Brazil. It was a time of humiliation for us, as even Crest toothpaste was regarded as a delicacy, as if it was some fancy spice from India. In any case, New York was filthy, dark, and rife with robberies during that period. From my dorm overlooking Morningside Park, I repeatedly saw elderly people being mugged. At that time, wallet theft was still ubiquitous.

The taxi left me at the school entrance at two in the morning. I had to prove to the guard that I was a new resident in the dorm. He let me in but warned that the room key was with the administrator and that I would have to wake him up. Naturally, waking him up infuriated him greatly. But then, with key in hand, I strolled through the old hall, adorned with paintings of all the former presidents of the institution. Their eyes followed me down that long, silent corridor with exaggeratedly high ceilings. Finally, I entered my room. There was no bed linen, but I was so tired that I lay down on the mattress and silently began to cry.

It was a few weeks before I remembered the parchment with the strange Kameoth. I started working in The Jewish Theological Seminary's library, and one day someone pointed out to me a kind of nobleman who was leafing through books: "That's the boss, the head librarian, Mr. Shmeltzer!" Being responsible for an academic library requires a learned appearance, I thought to myself.

When I saw him in the library again, I took courage and approached him. It was difficult to capture his attention; his eyes, fixed on what he was reading, only looked up when it became impossible to ignore me. Then he raised his eyes and, meeting mine, offered me the opening I needed: "I have some material that I brought from Brazil that I believe may be of value. I would like to show you."

He studied me for a few moments. Still absorbed in whatever

he was doing, and as if coming out of a trance, he replied, "Leave it here in the library office. I'll take a look later." His lack of interest was so obvious that it took me a few days to remember to leave the parchment.

They knocked on my door that same day, around eleven at night, to say that I had a phone call. We only had one telephone on the floor. I ran to the phone in my pajamas, fearing it might be terrible news. At that time of night, who could it be? I didn't know anyone in the city. Yes, it was Dr. Shmeltzer.

"Whose material is this?" he asked directly, as if interrogating me.

"Material?" I replied, realizing that the question was unnecessary. "Why?" I reacted, remembering the feeling I had had months before when I sensed that the parchment was something important.

He continued: "This material belongs to a parchment collection from sixteenth-century Turkey. It is rare and fits perfectly into a collection that we have here in the Rare Books Room. It is a Kabbalistic work depicting amulets for the most varied situations and contains rare Kameoth drawings. In fact, we are interested in keeping this material at the library and incorporating it into our collection!"

He paused for a second. "Is this material yours?" he then asked with a clear intention.

I'm rich!—I thought, already overcome with guilt because that material wasn't exactly mine. Still, certainly no one in Brazil, not even at school, would ever know. No record existed of it, let alone that I took it. There was nothing to fear. And, in any case, it would have ended up in the trash! All of this, I reasoned. But what came out of my mouth went the other way: "This material belongs to a school in Rio de Janeiro... But how much are we talking about?"

Dr. Shmeltzer then explained that although the item was valuable, there was no real market for it; an auctioneer would have to evaluate it. I immediately proposed to contact the school and get back to him about the situation. And so I did. After nearly two months, the school replied that the library in New York could keep the material as long as it had an inscription on the parchment stating the institution which had donated it.

Everyone was happy, and Dr. Shmeltzer divided a fictitious amount into several years, designating me as a donor so that I could deduct taxes related to my work at the library from these installments, something that, given my limited budget, would be of great help.

There are very mysterious things in Tijuca, but to understand them, you have to be contemplative. And I don't doubt that traveling with those *Kameoth*, with those amulets to open destiny, was providential for someone like me, vulnerable to the angels of uncertainty and restlessness.

SATAN IN FIRST CLASS

The amulets, I'm sure, protected me from a blow that came from the "other side," a term that Kabbalists used to talk about the world of obstacles. The word "Satan" derives from the root "to obstruct," and this is exactly what that angel—an intermediary in manifesting the shadows and ambivalences that clutter and obstruct the paths of life—does. The deeper and more significant the paths, the more deceitful the "creator of obstacles" becomes, and the more powers he possesses.

In the plane's luggage were the Kabbalistic scrolls that I mentioned earlier, as I traveled from Rio to New York. They were the ones who protected me from what I'm going to tell you now. I was flying to America to begin rabbinical studies, and I was apprehensive about the challenge: it was a new life in a country where I didn't know a soul.

The pessimistic version of Murphy's Law that says "everything that can go wrong will" is not a statistical truth, despite being a real representation of what will occur with some probability. Of course, the more expectations we have regarding a project or event, the more attentive we are to record moments when this possibility (within its humble statistics) can occur. When we are not paying attention, many moments in which things do not go wrong simply go unnoticed.

Then came this: "Passengers, this is the captain speaking. I want to inform you that Hurricane Emily is in the North Carolina region and that we will have to make a stopover in Miami to wait until weather conditions improve."

Anything but that! In two days, I would have to register at the school, and I still had several questions regarding my scholarship that needed clarifying. This new setback would bring a chain of inconveniences, and I was insecure enough already.

We landed, and I stayed at the hotel in Miami overnight. But the next day, unable to bear the anxiety any longer, I took my bags back to the airport. In the aftermath of hundreds of flights cancelled, I found complete chaos. The airport, just recently re-opened, would still take several days for all systems to normalize.

I was so terrified that I started crying profusely in front of the ticket attendant at the counter. I don't know what came over him—whether it was compassion or whether, thinking about it today, it was a big setup from the "other side"—but he looked at me and whispered "Don't tell anyone" in a complicit, quiet tone, "there's only one seat in first class, and I'm giving you an upgrade!"

I couldn't believe it! I went straight to the boarding gate, fearing that someone would come and question my stroke of luck. The annulment of fortune is a well-known phenomenon, and nothing is more painful than having your luck confiscated.

I sat in the first class window seat, as comfortable as a baby whose mother had tucked it into the crib. Heavy rain was still falling from the sky, but I looked at it through the window with a feeling of relief and comfort. I thought about my future; I imagined the safety of home and Brazil, while the storm made this young immigrant's journey more inhospitable. I desired solitude during that profound and introspective moment.

Then, the person who would sit next to me arrived in the aisle seat. He was a big man—more bulky than fat—and he dropped his body into the seat, producing quite a reverberation. He took up all possible space in the already privileged first class seat, even encroaching on my armrest. We understand how sacred these boundaries are, especially with a stranger!

Soon after he got more comfortable, and loosened his seatbelt, I felt that he wanted to start a conversation. I looked out the window, trying to avoid interaction. The last thing I wanted was to enter into a frugal, empty dialogue. My moment was sublime and personal.

I did everything I could to appear absent, but the guy was outgoing: he cleared his throat, turned towards me, and made some half-hearted interjection; in short, he made it clear that I wouldn't be able to rest until I answered him. I had to pay reluctant attention to his presence, bordering on antipathy. That was all he needed.

He asked, "You're from New York?" as if his ticket included such a privilege.

"No, I'm Brazilian," I said laconically and conclusively.

He then decided to make another sally move, this time through divination: "Are you going there to study?" as if in a chess game. I concluded with a dry "Yes" in an end-of-conversation tone.

But he continued: "How interesting... Do you have family in New York?"

"Neither family nor acquaintances"—I replied through my teeth, turning towards the window refuge.

"Nobody?"—he said in a tone of false astonishment.

My silence reaffirmed what I had said without having to repeat it. "And what are you going to study?" he asked, demonstrating that he would not give in so easily to surgical rebuttals.

At that moment, I thought that telling the stranger that I was going to start my studies to become a rabbi, in addition to exposing myself unnecessarily, would open up new fronts of curiosity and questions that would further engage me in an interaction from which I was trying to extricate myself at all costs. "Mechanical engineering," I said with an air of checkmate. What could be colder and more uninteresting than a specific technical area?

"Mechanical engineering?" he repeated with irritating interest. I wasn't lying; I was solely omitting, since to attend rabbinical school one must have completed an academic degree beforehand. For more than two thousand years, this custom of rabbis having another profession as a livelihood has persisted. Rabbis have been shoemakers, carpenters, doctors, and farmers; it was a way to prevent tradition and knowledge from becoming commodities. So it continues to this day. The seminary in New York required another degree as a prerequisite. Having made significant progress in my engineering studies, I had managed to convince Columbia University to accept my Brazilian credits, allowing me to complete my degree concurrently with my rabbinic studies.

"Which university?" he resumed with renewed enthusiasm. I suddenly realized I had made a mistake but couldn't pinpoint exactly where.

"Columbia University..." I replied suspiciously.

He then exclaimed with the amazement so typical of a coincidence: "I can't believe it! I am familiar with everyone in Columbia's Mechanical Engineering Department. The dean himself is a personal friend of mine. I will write a letter of recommendation for you!" He immediately began looking for a pen and paper.

The plane had, by then, taken off. My seatmate unfolded the table and began writing a long letter to the dean. In the text, he introduced me as a personal friend asking him to help me in any way possible.

Of course, I began wondering who this new and inopportune friend could be. And as he finished the letter, he began to tell me about himself: "I am vice president of General Electric. My private jet had problems due to the hurricane and I had to take this commercial flight. I've got a nose for these things. I knew there was a reason for this type of inconvenience." He seemed sure of some puzzle he had solved.

"You know what... I like people like you!" he said, leaving me confused about his line of reasoning. What qualities could I possess to cultivate such empathy? He continued: "I like courageous people who are not afraid to face a new country and a new culture and go head-to-head to face its challenges. This is the spirit of

America! And you know what else?"—he interrupted, as if about to surprise even himself—"I'm going to give you your first job here in America!"

Then he repeated this again, taking a business card from his pocket: "This is my card. Here you have my contact details. The bottom one is my secretary, Sandy's. As soon as you organize yourself, look for her and ask her to speak to me, just saying you are the 'boy on the plane.' I have already given you your first job!"

I started to feel something macabre and sinister. That was the impossible opposite of Murphy's Law. How many people would dream of having a godfather and protector like this? But for me, it was of no use. I began to distrust this quirk of fate. I started to imagine that choices like mine—for the sacred and the search for studies in the spiritual field—might need to face this type of ordeal. Could he be a "messenger" sent to confuse me? Is he trying to dissuade me by promising occult benefits? Could this seduction be an obstacle along my path? I then became certain that I had evidence. Of course, Satan would travel first class!

Perhaps my heightened sensitivity at that moment led to all of this, but the interaction seemed highly intentional. Although the hurricane's unintentional events sparked the interaction, it appeared as though numerous elements had come together to create a cohesive design or plan. That man's appearance, soft talk, and excessive enthusiasm made him seem like a demon. He might also have had a sexual interest in the unprotected young man, but I hadn't yet deciphered this.

Situated on the boundaries between the real and the supernatural, it is possible that my still-naive self understood the episode from the wrong point of view. However, as a neophyte of a spiritual tradition, my interpretation was not so beyond reason. That's precisely how I interpreted the event. After all, the occult and extra-natural always intersect with reality and fantasy. As previously mentioned, this is not mere quackery or trickery, but rather sometimes the convergence of parallel realities.

I kept the letter to the dean, but I never used it.

As for the business card with my obstructive angel's contacts, I kept it for many years.

Frustrated, Satan never received a call from his secretary about the boy on the plane. Of course, there were the *Kameoth*—the amulets I had in the plane's cargo—that protected me. After all, weren't they talismans to guarantee my path? Antidotes for roadblocks? I've always heard that evil aims to obstruct, never relying on physically blocking a way, but rather in deceiving someone into going the wrong direction.

This angel's actions also always occur through reward strategies, rather than by creating explicit obstacles. Wrong paths can lead to much greater harm than simple prohibitions. And bad choices are much more disruptive than the challenges of possible blockages. One stops us; the other takes us far away.

A third observer might tell the story differently of what happened between me and the man on that plane, but it was like this, with shudders and astonishment, that it lodged in my memory. Was it all due to a heightened sensitivity on my part, or perhaps some form of fantasy? Those are questions that will remain unanswered in zones beyond my imagination.

When two women sit at a crossroads, one on one side and one on the other, looking at each other, it is clear that they are performing witchcraft. What can you do? If you are with someone else, hold hands and, without looking, say, "Agrat, Ozlat, Uzia, and Beluzia were extinguished with a dark arrow!"

TALMUD PES. 111TH

THE BAR MITZVAH POLTERGEIST

Rites of passage exist to mark the most important existential crossroads in our lives. They function to encompass the feelings and senses that emerge on these occasions.

Patrick appeared in my diary with the following note from my secretary: "Bar Mitzvah, morning service of November 14, 1987, *Parsha Vayera*." (That Hebrew transliterated phrase refers to the excerpt from the weekly reading of the Torah which the boy was responsible for preparing.)

It was an ordinary day, and I had already had a few routine meetings. I met people grappling with marital problems and child-related issues, while others sought guidance on matters related to litigation or illness; the ordinary events of life that take on extraordinary significance as we experience them. And so I got ready to welcome Patrick and his parents to their first meeting for the bar mitzvah, the coming-of-age ceremony that boys usually undergo at thirteen, and girls—a bat mitzvah—often at the age of twelve.

However, if anything is "not ordinary," it is precisely a bar mitzvah. Following the tradition, which requires a boy to sing and perform rituals in front of the nuclear family, extended family, and friends—all together in one space—is no small feat. In addition to the challenges of celebration, this is a phase of puberty during which the voice deepens, adapts to a rapidly growing body, and internally adjusts to hormone changes. Such a transition is often accompanied by psychological, psychic, and social upheaval as well.

The door opened, and, together with my secretary, the boy's

parents entered. But, contrary to what was customary, the boy stayed outside. The parents said that they would like to talk to me before he joined us. I accepted these conditions with some curiosity. The father then stood up and spoke.

"Rabbi, we wanted to speak to you before Patrick came in because we're having difficulties with him. These issues are not trivial, and I'm at a loss for words." Then, sitting down, he continued: "Strange events have been occurring in our house, and we think they are related to Patrick."

"Events of what kind?"—I interrupted.

"Supernatural events—objects, glasses breaking, and many other inexplicable events," the shaken father said, observing my reaction.

"But why do you associate this with Patrick?"

"Why? Because this is what typically happens when he arrives at places. It's always about him. We've gotten used to it, although we're scared. We think that, perhaps, the bar mitzvah can bring him closer to religion and the sacred, making it all stop. Please, God!"

"Let's go step by step. How is Patrick at school? What's his life like?"

For the first time, the mother spoke.

"He is very closed, Rabbi. He has few friends, and it is difficult to convince him to go out, do sports, etcetera. He is very shy and reserved. We hope your conversation with him and preparation for the bar mitzvah will help him get over this. For us, it is very difficult. The maid is also terrified, and she wants to leave. I still have our youngest, Alan, who is only three years old. I can barely keep up with things. I'm so worried!"

"What types of situations have occurred?" I asked, trying to hide my disbelief.

The mother took the lead again. "When he gets angry, for example, things break or move. One day, a cup broke in my hand; the windows and walls of the house cracked. Things simply shatter.

They break, Rabbi! Appliances burn, and light bulbs explode. This isn't even the most important thing, but the fact is that we are incurring huge losses, and we don't know what to do. We've already sent him to psychoanalysts and relaxation therapies, but nothing has helped."

German translates the term *Poltergeist* as "noisy ghost" (*poltern* = noisy; *Geist* = ghost or spirit). Poltergeist describes a range of supernatural phenomena, including sudden lights, moving objects, abnormalities in electrical and telephone installations, audible noises, and toys that function even without batteries. It is believed that the focus of this disorder is a child in puberty, generally female. The extrasensory faculty that enables the mind to directly act on matter is known as psychokinesis, derived from the Greek words *psyché* (soul) and *kinein* (move).

Suddenly, I woke up to the real world: No, it can't be. They are in shock. I have to maintain my composure, I thought. I'm a rabbi, and you're here at a difficult time. I can't become part of this story!

It was clear something was going on, and they needed help. However, I never thought of the supernatural as the first item in a field of possibilities. Everything pointed to a general picture of a boy with problems and issues typical of that difficult stage of life. I thought, after a good conversation with Patrick, I will know how to guide things so that we can take advantage of the bar mitzvah and support him.

I asked Patrick's parents to now let me talk to him alone. The parents looked at each other with some resistance but gave in. They left my office, and Patrick entered. Looking down, he sat on the chair in front of my desk, remaining still without looking at me.

I thought about what I would say, and before I could introduce myself and greet him, I heard a dry splitting sound. I spun around quickly enough to witness what had just happened: The glass covering two of my framed diplomas hanging on the side wall had cracked diagonally, from corner to corner. I can safely say that there had been no crack in the glass until that moment, and I saw the crack advancing across both frames until the split in one vertex met the other. It seemed like the glass couldn't resist pressure at the frames' ends.

A mysterious silence then took over between Patrick and me. He didn't even look at the cracked glass. I waited a few moments to see if he would confirm what had happened, but he didn't move at all. I confess I was scared. I was not exactly terrified by the event itself, which seemed supernatural, but by the situation I had before me. I was looking for any other eyewitnesses with whom I could share a "Did you see that?!"

But since Patrick didn't offer me this partnership, I decided to open our conversation without mentioning the incident: "Hi, I'm Rabbi Nilton Bonder. I'll be with you as you prepare for your bar mitzvah." I pondered his thoughts as I spoke.

He nodded without looking in my direction. I tried a few more sentences to explain our plan and process. Still, I couldn't even get him to nod. I did my best to start a conversation, but without success. Then I attempted to be empathetic with silence of my own. Then I asked a few questions about how he felt. Still, he kept silent.

I accepted Patrick's silence; in fact, I stayed in his company for a few endless minutes in precisely that way. At one point, in his first independent action, he looked at me sternly. So, I asked if he was angry. He didn't answer. I'd never felt so disarmed and deprived of the possibility of penetrating such thick armor. I inquired if he had any thoughts or concerns about his bar mitzvah, and if there was anything I could do to support him. Nothing. The boy remained impassive. Finally, defeated, I told him I would ask his parents to come back in. When I got up, he said, "I'll do it!" and went back to looking at the floor.

The parents entered and immediately noticed the cracked glass over the diplomas. They looked at each other but didn't say anything to me. I told them that Patrick had told me he would do the bar mitzvah, and I began to address them as if I were talking to the boy. I explained we had a teacher who was really cool, and that we would have a whole year to do everything calmly. Then, looking at the parents, I added, "We are one year away from the ceremony. It is a very intense year for the boys; they change profoundly throughout this period. Patrick will grow a lot, I'm sure."

At the first opportunity, Patrick left the room, allowing me to speak privately with his parents once more. I decided to tell them the Hasidic story of parents who bring their troubled, rebellious son to the rabbi, who advises them to "Love him even more! And to love more is to pay more attention." I said this while looking into the mother's eyes.

Finally, I managed to calm them both down by reminding them that we had two invaluable allies: a wonderful, caring teacher, and time—a whole year of preparation. It was clear that they should continue with Patrick's therapist and therapy, but it was also important that they did not use the religious space to solve problems in the afterlife. Being partners in this sense, and assisting each other with problems that pertain to this life, or this world, would be far more beneficial than exploring the occult. When we are talking about ourselves and our lives, perhaps we want to venture into the meanings of the supernatural order. However, when it comes to a child's life, it is irresponsible to enter symbolic or esoteric regions that we have no understanding of.

It didn't seem to me that we were dealing with a web of past lives, or beings from another dimension. Patrick indeed seemed disturbed, but he was most likely entangled in the psychophysical emotions that usually occur at this time of life. He'd grow out of it. Still, is it any wonder that parents sometimes see Poltergeist phenomena associated with puberty in their children?

And so it was. As I imagined, our bar mitzvah teacher created a powerful bond with the boy, and she was crucial in his development toward the big day. And just as water is the universal solvent, time is the universal elucidator: the bar mitzvah went smoothly, and Patrick behaved as expected. He was taller and more talkative, then, compared to that first afternoon in my office. He had radically transformed from the serious and gloomy boy I had first met.

Two things, however, caught my attention. In the middle of the ceremony, a cat appeared out of nowhere and walked over the pipes of the synagogue's old organ. Everyone found it curious and "cute," whereas I exchanged glances with the parents.

The second incident then went unnoticed: I was facing the audience, which did not fill all the rows on the first floor of the synagogue. On the mezzanine, where some nannies were conversing and tending to children, one of them failed to notice a baby regurgitating on her shoulder. I watched as a stream of spray fell onto the first floor below, landing on empty chairs in one of the back rows. Neither the nanny nor anyone else saw this, as they were all looking towards us on the bimah.

Why did I find that strange? I don't think it was the associations with films like *The Exorcist*—which haunted me. On the contrary, I think it was the physical sensation of life—which, as children, we know so well—of rejecting and vomiting, as a reflexive act, from the depths of our bowels. That seemed to me a more suitable representation of a Poltergeist.

I will never, however, forget the look on that boy's face in my office. Its intensity was so overwhelming and so opaque that it exquisitely portrayed the dull and cloudy nature of a soul at that liminal moment of life. I congratulated Patrick on that celebratory day one year later. I did so as I did every bar and bat mitzvah, "*Mazal tov!*" which means "Good luck to you!"—or, more literally, "Have a favorable destiny!"

Rav said to Rabbi Chiya, "I saw an Arab take a sword and cut his camel in half. Soon after, he hit a tambourine. And the camel stood up whole, without any cuts! Rabbi Chiya asked Rav, "But did blood or dung come out when he cut it?" Rav replied, "No, there was nothing!" Rabbi Hyia said, "Since there was none, it must have been an optical illusion!"

TALMUD SAN. 67B

OPERATING WITH DR. FRITZ

Alexandre called with a serious and hollow voice. It wasn't clear to me whether it was due to the nature of the conversation, or whether he was avoiding anyone overhearing him. I knew he was having health problems, but I didn't have any further details.

"Nilton, I have a big problem. I have a malignant tumor on my neck. I'm terrified... I'm undergoing numerous tests in preparation for surgery... I was thinking about something, and you're the right person to help me."

"Alexandre, whatever I can do, my friend. How can I help you?"

"Here's the thing: I've already contacted a certain guy. Have you heard of Dr. Fritz? The doctor who performs spiritual operations?"

Dr. Fritz was a well-known character, then, among Brazilians. In the 1950s, a medium named Zé Arigó first came to light; he performed medical care and spiritual surgeries, speaking with a German accent, claiming to channel a spirit called Dr. Adolf Fritz, a German doctor who died in the First World War. Since then, other individuals had come forward to embody this Dr. Fritz.

"I've heard about him..."

"He's a doctor from Recife, and I've heard excellent things about him. I've already contacted him, and he seemed fine. I'm arranging for him to come to Rio to meet me. I'm paying a lot of money, including the ticket and accommodation. Do you think this is a crazy idea? I am terrified, but he's a physician, right? I am assuming he's legit."

"Alexandre, I don't know him. Naturally, I understand your concern. You aren't going to quit your medications to focus on this, are you?"

"No, of course not." He paused, and then added, "But I'm apprehensive about this operation, even though numerous people have praised this doctor for his exceptional qualities. You know he solved the singer Alcione's problem?—which was identical to my own."

Alexandre went on. "I will do everything correctly as my doctor prescribed, and prepare for my hospital operation. However, Fritz is coming to Rio on Wednesday."

"The day after tomorrow?"

"Yes—everything is ready for the operation, so we must act quickly. But since I'm fearful, I want someone I trust to be by my side."

I nodded.

"I didn't say anything to my wife," Alexandre continued. "I decided to move quickly, without even informing her. But I need someone there with me! I thought of you. Will you come? This Wednesday morning."

I was apprehensive. What if something goes wrong? I wondered. Furthermore, it occurred to me that this could potentially be medically illegal, and that, as a rabbi, I would be involved in something that would have significant religious and faith implications. Not to mention the fact that there is an explicit prohibition in Judaism against resorting to magicians and healers, even while some Talmud passages permit the use of any medical intervention in life-threatening situations.

For example, in one well-known Talmudic passage, a snake bites Ben Dama, and he quarrels with his uncle, Rabbi Ishmael, who declares that seeking healing from a healer is forbidden because it is a form of idolatry. Ben Dama begs his uncle, "Ishmael, allow me to receive treatment from this man! Then, I'll provide proof that the Scriptures permit it!" But he does not have time to finish his speech, because he dies. Rabbi Ishmael then declares before his body: "How fortunate are you, Ben Dama, that your body departed pure and your soul untouched, without having transgressed the words of your peers: 'He that diggeth a pit shall fall into it; and whosoever breaketh an hedge, a serpent shall bite him.'" (Ecclesiastes 10:8, King James Version)

Upon reflection, it's intriguing that the Talmud's text acknowledges the irony inherent in the narrative: "But hasn't he already experienced a snake's bite?" Clearly, the text conveys the ambiguity that the issue presents by introducing intellectual discussions that do not meet the needs of a dying person. Furthermore, snakes symbolize the reasoning of the human mind, which often indulges in transgressions...

Suddenly, I snapped out of my reverie and responded to Alexandre: "Okay, but what exactly will take place?"

He said, "Ah, that's good! You don't know what this means to me!"

I thought, it means that a rabbi is endorsing your act and that you are free from any guilt since you have rabbinic approval! Despite this bothering me, I continued listening and participating in the plan.

"I thought we could pick him up at the airport," Alexandre said. "You would come with me. Then we'll go to the hotel I booked for Dr. Fritz. I secured a room for my operation. And when it's over, I'll also stay there, resting for a while, until I can go home."

I was quiet.

"You'll be there with me the whole time," Alexandre said. "I'll feel safer having you with me. Great! You have no idea what this means to me. I can't thank you enough!"

When the call ended, I felt both trapped by Alexandre and sympathetic towards him. I was aware that if something went wrong, I would be in trouble both from a legal point of view—for participating in an act of quackery—and from a religious point of view—for endorsing the controversial issue of seeking spiritual treatments in a case like this. Rabbi Ishmael's "contentment" with the death of his nephew (who had lost his life but preserved his immaterial integrity) remained ever-present in my consciousness.

Then came the beautiful November morning when we picked up Dr. Edson Cavalcante Queiroz at the airport, and headed to a five-star hotel on the Copacabana beachfront. Alexandre introduced me as his rabbi to the doctor from Recife. Immediately, there was a moment of tension: Dr. Edson didn't know what a rabbi was; he had never heard that word! I was apprehensive about that. How come a doctor hadn't heard of a rabbi?

We entered the reserved hotel room, and Dr. Edson asked Alexandre to lie down on the bed and meditate. He went to the bathroom, where he started taking things out of his leather case, very 1980s doctor style. Alexandre was livid with the colors that chromatically characterize fear. He looked at me several times, quietly saying, "Nilton, I'm scared to death!" I tried to calm him down, as if I were sure of what we were doing.

Dr. Edson re-entered the room and said to Alexandre, "Let's begin. You're going to stay there very still, and we're going to anesthetize you. And I'm going to ask the rabbi—he's a rabbi, right?—to help me concentrate."

Alexandre obeyed as if following orders from another world. And, pale as he was, he began to calm down, taking on a cadaverous serenity. I was scared, and felt like I was in a surgical room filled with the odor of ether that Dr. Edson (or Fritz) rubbed on his hands. I believe it was still Dr. Edson, as he informed me immediately.

"Rabbi, let's pray together so that I can incorporate the spirit of Dr. Fritz."

I waited for more directions, but they didn't come. Meanwhile, Dr. Edson began to recite, or almost hum, some hymns. The repeated mentions of Jesus indicated their Christian content. With the best of intentions, I closed my eyes and attempted to facilitate a blessing for my friend.

This agony lasted a half hour, during which Alexandre was static. Given that he had been in a state of panic just a short while ago, I must admit that his calmness was impressive. He appeared to be under anesthesia.

Suddenly, the doctor (we're still allowing him that title) began to snort and make spasmodic movements. His eyes widened, and his sentences grew shorter: "Let's begin!" And, standing up, he gave the order, "You help me!"

I was terrified, but had the strength to remain composed. Then, suddenly, I exclaimed in German: *"Ich weiß nicht, ob ich helfen kann!"* "I don't know if I can help!"

I'd studied the language for two years, and during that time I also studied Yiddish, believing that both languages would yield benefits. After all, Yiddish is a dialect of German. But I was mistaken. One thing got in the way of the other: I went to German class at Berlitz in Leblon, and, when I was about to speak, a Yiddish construction came out that provoked strange looks from the teacher. They weren't errors per se, but old-fashioned ways of speaking.

Dr. Fritz (I imagine it was already him!) looked at me strangely. I became scared. Did he understand my Yiddish? I wondered. No, he clearly didn't understand what I was saying.

I felt a little empowered, at first, at his not-knowing, but then the doubts flooded back in. Was this guy an impostor? A charlatan about to put Alexandre's life (and my reputation) at risk? What about my German-Yiddish—was it be possible that Dr. Fritz no longer knew his native language? Did he somehow unlearn, when taking up his new occult vernacular? Or would Dr. Fritz simply decline to engage in my act of disbelief, seeing it perhaps as a kind of "bait" I'd thrown in the water? At that moment, I was opting for this last possibility.

Because he scared me. His face was all contorted. There was no smile or kindness. Everything was abrupt.

"Take the case," he said, interrupting my thoughts. I got it.

"Open it!" I opened it. Inside were huge needles, with heads similar to those thumbtacks we used to put on maps to mark a location.

He took the case from my hands and inserted one of the needles. Then he moved the needle closer to Alexandre's neck, in the area where the tumor was likely located. Then he lightly stuck the needle through Alexandre's skin as if he were going to start an acupuncture session. The needle, however, was huge and thick. He pressed the neck skin to the point where a small droplet of blood formed. "Hold this!" he told me.

Do you know the moment when you realize you've gotten yourself into trouble? I kept thinking about how I could get out of this. What if something was about to go seriously wrong? Now, I was undoubtedly involved.

I glanced at Alexandre, who by this time had a large needle inserted in his neck. He was still serene, indifferent to everything that was happening. I feared disrupting his crucial process while simultaneously fearing his potential harm. Had he called me with the expectation that I would protect him? Or did he expect faith in me to fuel the whole process?

It was a matter of seconds, not more than two or three, and I found myself helping the doctor push the needle. It entered the neck and absorbed the drop of blood that had appeared. Alexandre's skin remained clear, even though the needle was completely buried at a depth of some ten or fifteen millimeters. There was not even a sign of redness. It didn't seem normal to me that the needle had entered Alexandre's body without any apparent sign of injury. What's more troubling, I couldn't understand how Alexandre could remain so serene and placid.

We repeated this needle-insertion ritual a dozen times, if not more. The doctor inserted most of them, but now and then he would say, "Press down!" and I would join in. At these moments, there was always a dense silence—that is, during the needle penetration I was handling.

For a few endless minutes, Dr. Fritz left Alexandre looking like Frankenstein. Then he slowly removed the needles and asked me to do the same as if they were an essential part of this blessing. I was unsure whether any other "natural person" had ever held that "honor" before me. Perhaps my title, which the doctor had just discovered, bestowed this honor upon me. Throughout the entire process, I felt as though he was mocking me, and I anticipated a playful wink that never materialized, particularly because my participation resembled a magic act where a member of the audience was summoned onto the stage—in this case, to ensure that the needles were not flexible.

Again Dr. Fritz sat down, and, after a series of deep breaths, took on the persona of Dr. Edson. In reality, the same individual either had a different appearance or was a different person altogether. In the physical world, a single individual wore the same attire, yet a metamorphosis occurred in the mind.

Dr. Edson told me that Alexandre would sleep for another half hour or so and that he would go to his room because he was exhausted from the trip and surgery.

Indeed, Alexandre slept soundly, and when he woke up, wondered what had happened. I described the events that had transpired. He seemed very impressed that all this could have happened this way—while he was there, absent, abducted by mere suggestion.

I finally left after making sure that my friend was okay. There were no marks on his neck. He was simply amazed, and remained introspective about everything I told him.

It was a few days later when I discovered the doctors had canceled the scheduled operation. Alexandre had redone the exams and his tumor had not completely disappeared but had shrunk substantially, much to the perplexity of the physicians and the rest of us.

Alexandre is out there, still. Now and then, I see him. However, concerning Dr. Edson, it was only two years after his election as deputy for Pernambuco's state government that he was murdered by the caretaker of his country house. I no longer follow the curious character to discover if there has been an afterlife, of yet another person operating out there as Dr. Fritz. I also wonder if Dr. Edson's diploma was recognized by the heavenly bodies.

Joking aside, I don't know what I experienced that day. The procedure's efficacy and results were astonishing, that is undeniable. However, the conduct of the médium and the entire staging had moments of primality, as if I had participated in amateur theatrics. Ben Dama would argue with his uncle: "Look, I told you!" Even so, Ben Dama's uncle maintained an adherence to his chosen path of focused and unshaken faith. Within the frailty and finitude of humans, we've all been bitten by the serpent's bite.

MARRIAGE OF DESTINY

It is traditionally believed that arranging a *shidduch*, or assuming the role of a matchmaker, will earn you special recognition in heaven. This comes from a blessing you offer someone when finding them a mate. Of course, we are referring to the classic or ancient model, a system based on the idea of finding a partner who lasts a lifetime—in fact, this is the origin of the word shidduch, which means "tranquility."

Such a comfort today may seem anachronistic. Still, it's common for us to harbor dreams and fantasies about our significant other, particularly due to the distressing nature of the constant search for a partner. These feelings are also present in other decisions, including those related to work. Wouldn't it be comforting to have a clear and definitive position forever? Later on, we might fantasize about leaving our jobs, but that's a different story.

Marcia was the next appointment on my agenda. There was no specified topic in my notes for her visit. Generally, my secretary makes every effort to obtain information about scheduled interviews, but she often faces resistance when people assert their inalienable right to silence, citing "personal" reasons for meeting with the rabbi.

She was, I believe, under thirty years old, and a lovely woman. At first, she didn't talk about marriage or the search for a partner, at least not explicitly. And she quickly explained: "Rabbi, thank you for receiving me. The fact that I'm going to live in Australia is what brings me here."

"Great!"—I reacted spontaneously. "When I was a child, my parents almost emigrated to Australia. At that time, immigration procedures were relatively simple, and I recall visiting the consulate with my parents. During our visit, my mother attempted to entice me with the prospect of a new future using kangaroos as a motivator."

Marcia smiled. "Really? In my case, I am going there for work, and will stay for three or four years. Then we'll see what the future brings." She paused, looking out the window, then back at me.

"Well, let me get straight to the point," she continued. "I came here today because I'm traveling alone. I don't know anyone in this part of the world and I thought that if I could leave Brazil with a recommendation for a synagogue in Australia, that might help me when I arrive. You know how it is—it's always beneficial to be part of a community. It opens many doors."

"For sure! I must say that I don't personally know any rabbis in Australia. But I can look in this directory." I reached behind me and grabbed a book from a shelf. "It's a Conservative Movement catalog that lists all the rabbis and locations."

Marcia seemed a little disappointed. It is common for rabbis to offer references in similar situations, but I had never had any contact with Australian Judaism. Still, I took the book that contained the addresses and contacts of rabbis from all over the world and searched for Australia. I asked Marcia, "What city?"

"Melbourne."

Several synagogues in Melbourne were listed. My list contained only the Conservative synagogues; that's the movement to which I belong. I started to eliminate them by location until I saw a name that looked familiar.

"Wait a second," I said aloud, seeing the familiar name. "I believe Denis was a colleague of mine. If he's who I think he is, his synagogue would be great for you. I remember Denis as a nice guy. He can probably help. It says here his synagogue is in East Melbourne."

Marcia was enthusiastic, saying that East Melbourne wasn't far from where she would be staying. So I copied Denis' name for her, even though I was still unsure if he was who I thought he was. His name had a prefix of "Dr." I imagined it would be a doctorate—a common title among rabbis, but I didn't know for sure.

Marcia took the small piece of paper on which I wrote the rabbi's name and the congregation address. She thanked me, and I wished her success. Then she left my office to cross the oceans and live on the other side of the planet. I thought I would never hear from her again.

The rest of my afternoon was filled with meetings that would completely erase the somewhat innocuous interaction of offering search services in telephone directories, which is how we did things once upon a time before Google.

I remember, however, that shortly after Marcia left, I went to look for the names of former colleagues on another list and found Denis there also, even though the surname was different. But since the mission to deliver a synagogue was by then complete, I let it go.

Many years passed, and during an afternoon of similar interviews in my office—as if fate had just twirled the wheel of time, defining closures—Marcia appeared on the list that day. By name alone, I wouldn't have remembered her, and even if I had remembered the exchange we had about Australia, I would have had no reason to believe this Marcia was the same as the one years earlier.

A moment later, Marcia entered my office with a broad smile. "Remember me?"

I recognized the face, but I didn't know immediately from where, or who it was. Faced with my hesitation, she continued: "Don't you remember? I'm Marcia, and I was here about eight years ago when I was going to live in Australia. Remember? Do you remember when you gave me the name of a certain rabbi and a synagogue address in Melbourne?"

When she mentioned the searching through the rabbis list,

it immediately brought back the memory. "Yes, of course," I said, "but has it already been that long—eight years?!"

"Rabbi, I'm only in Rio now for a few days, visiting family, but I couldn't help but stop by and tell you the crazy story that happened to me. Look here..."

She then showed photos of what appeared to be her husband and two young children, who were very cute.

"All of this, Rabbi, is the outcome of our conversation!"

"Really?" I replied, already envisioning she had met someone in that synagogue, eventually getting married and starting a family.

"Yes. Let me tell you the story," she said, settling comfortably into the chair in front of me.

"That day, when you gave me a piece of paper with the name of the rabbi and the synagogue's address, I kept it. However, life has its priorities and vicissitudes, and I never in fact went to that synagogue. I ended up moving to another place, and life went on.

"And there, a family invited me to dinner at their house. It was there that I met a young man, a doctor.

"We became friends, and the relationship progressed into romance. I was dating this doctor for some time—I think for a couple of months already, when one fine day, Rabbi, I'm at home cleaning and I find that piece of paper in my pants pocket... Just the one you gave me!"

"And what's strange about that?" I asked, eager to delve into the tale of a thousand and one nights.

"That was my boyfriend's name, Rabbi!"

"No way!"

"Yes. It was the same name as the young man I was dating. I couldn't believe it. It wasn't a common name, so the simple law of probability could explain it. But I thought, *How can it be? My boyfriend isn't a rabbi; he's a doctor.*

"I hurried to talk to him—my boyfriend—to show him the

paper, and I told him the story, saying, 'Look how crazy it is! It's your namesake!' And to my total surprise, he suddenly became emotional and declared, 'No, it's not a similar name; it's me!'

"He went on to explain that he had started his rabbinical studies but that he later changed careers and devoted himself to medicine. Furthermore, he explained that before completing his medical residency, he had worked some time at that synagogue as a rabbi."

"But didn't you already know that about him? I mean, hadn't he told you about himself?" I interrupted, trying to put the pieces together.

"He explained to me that this was no longer the axis of his life, that it had been something temporary, a side job, and that he ended up not telling me anything about this side of himself simply because there hadn't been an opportunity to do so, yet. After all, we had only been together a short time, and that part of his past was not that relevant anymore."

I then remembered the prefix "Dr." next to his name in the directory. How strange the human mind is! Marcia, herself the protagonist, had slipped my mind, but even today, the listing with "Dr." of that name jogged in my memory like a photogram!

"And then?" I asked, returning from the reveries of my thoughts to a reality that sometimes proves more daring than fantasies themselves.

"Then, I took it as a sign. I had to marry this person. Rabbi, I left Rio de Janeiro with his name in my pocket. In a different city, I encountered a man in a random house whose name matched the one you had written on that small piece of paper. I thought this was magical! I believed you were an improbable angel, capable of bringing about an unlikely, if not impossible, encounter.

"So I married him, and we are happy." Then she added, sweetly, pointing to her children in the photograph, "This is Paulo, and this is Guilherme.

"I couldn't help but tell you this story. You made the quintessential shidduch! You solved an equation having only variables! You gave me the name of my husband, whom I didn't know and who lived across the planet, as an address I never went to, but the heavens arranged our meeting. In fact, here is the very paper you gave me that day!" she concluded, showing and pointing to that small piece of paper, a passcode of opening destinies written on a monotonous afternoon of routine.

After a hug and many thanks, she left my office once again.

I was left thinking about all those coincidences. Was it destiny? What value did she assign to that burlesque sequence, akin to a B-film, when she unraveled this plot? Did she define her destiny simply by, "I took it as a sign"—this must be the man? Or are there really "links" outside the plans we make for ourselves? Links we don't see, and therefore cannot put all the pieces together.

What left me most thoughtful, though, was the latent power of the routine. How is it possible that such an ordinary and commonplace moment could produce warps in time and destiny of this magnitude? How could a sleepy afternoon and a trivial gesture have such an impact on life, inducing such strange crossroads of destiny?

This is the power, the torque, attainable at every moment. Do you recognize those everyday, routine moments? They have impressive incubative abilities!

In the city of Pozen, a family moved into a large stone house. There was a sealed basement in it, and everyone respected the prohibition on entering it until, one day, the teenage son decided to unlock the door and go down. The discovery of that boy's dead body on the stairs marked the beginning of a demon invasion, there. Strange noises, and mysterious thrown objects began tormenting the family, too.

They asked the Baal Shem Tov to resolve the situation. He questioned the demons, who said they had a right to the house and would bring the matter to the rabbinical court. Despite the unusual circumstances, they convened a court and presented their case. According to them, the house's previous owner had a relationship with a beautiful female demon, and from their union, a son was born. However, the wife then discovered her husband having an affair with the demon, and she summoned an exorcist to expel them. But faced with the request, the owner decided to allow the demons to live in the basement from that moment on.

The final verdict determined that demons could not live in cities, that their place was in the mountains or valleys, and that there was no consistent legal claim in their allegation. They then called an exorcist and closed the case.

KAV YAKAR, RABBI TSI KAIDANOVER
(LATE SEVENTEENTH CENTURY)

TALMUD AND THE SOUND OF SILENCE

Following on the idea of my routine's latent powers, it makes sense to tell you about an event right after I arrived in the United States to begin my studies.

To live abroad in a big city before the digital age presented challenges. Connections were difficult and expensive. In the pre-internet era, the simple rumor of a malfunctioning telephone on the Columbia University campus could gain widespread attention and create a rush to that particular public phone, where inserting a single quarter would allow unlimited international calls.

I always suspected the telephone company's consent, as it defied logic to remain clandestine or continue for such a long time without detection. Regardless, it's important to note that individuals who engage in illegal activities consistently exhibit civility and helpfulness, fostering a sense of empathy with others involved. Thus, each of us had the right to our turn for at most ten minutes, and everyone respected the rules with a worthy sense of urbanity and politeness.

I didn't know anyone in New York outside the school. This wasn't a problem on weekdays when I was involved in my studies. On weekends, however, it was different. Not to mention, how challenging it felt during holidays when people would travel to see their families or engage in activities with their friendship networks.

It wasn't exactly loneliness that I felt (which is more of a state, a circumstance of life), but isolation that created a sense of need and, I confess, had me somehow embarrassed. I have difficulty with feelings of vulnerability. I love empathy, but I hate commiseration!

It always hits me like a disdain, a judgment, or a label of my fate and existential condition.

One sympathizer I tolerated, however, was a renowned professor—a luminary in the Talmud department, the most prestigious in a rabbinical school. I will call him Professor Leonard. He was an eccentric. He was a scholar of Judaism's most classic text, having published various books and serving as the dean in matters of jurisprudence and ethics. He was single, a bachelor, someone who presented himself that way as part of his identity.

His fame filled the seminary. Academic environments excel at building stereotypes, and his was unusual. His fame came also from his very conservative political positions, and he was a personal friend of the current U.S. president. However, what truly characterized him was a certain sloppiness: he consistently had breadcrumbs on the lapel of his suit, or even in his abundant beard, akin to a neglected garden.

There were also suspicions about his love life and conjectures about his sexual identity. These were times marked by prejudice, or perhaps a combination of puritanism, chaste theatricality, and profuse talk, conspicuous features of religious settings.

On the first Saturday after my arrival, I didn't think his invitation to lunch at his house could be suspicious. He was fluent in Spanish, and when confronted with a Brazilian at a school where the only people of color were Americans, and a few Canadians, I took his gesture simply as one of welcome and inclusivity.

The students' perception of his eccentricity was entirely based on imagination, although I did once witness in the cafeteria: while he was pulling something out of his pocket, he dropped a peepshow token, which spun a bit on the floor until it landed next to the buffet table. Times Square peepshows consisted of pornographic photographs or objects viewed through a hole in a wall by people sitting, usually alone, in dark private spaces. By that time, they had turned into booths, where one bought tokens and used them to watch nudity and sex scenes.

I still remember the silence in the cafeteria at that moment, until a student approached the token, picked it up, and handed it back to the teacher, who didn't even appear embarrassed.

I went to some of these lunches at his house, and I confess that they were quite boring, with talk about teachers I didn't know and topics that didn't interest me, all in the melancholy light of a late summer afternoon in New York. However, he prepared the meal with refinement—with many items that exceeded my budget—and was also genuinely concerned about my situation. I believe our two characters, one vulnerable at the opening and the other at the closing of life, reflected not only my isolation but also his loneliness.

His house was spacious—the biggest and most sophisticated of those I visited during my student period. All my acquaintances lived in dorms or modest suites, often with astronomical rents. His house was solid, similar to those of most American university professors, typical of those who earn more than they spend. Several catalogs of gadgets and inventions sat upon a table, and there was a bizarre portable sauna in his bedroom opposite the bed. The sauna, akin to a telephone booth, accommodated only one individual and plugged into an electrical outlet. When I saw it for the first time, I caught myself imagining what it would be like to use the strange device, but I quickly tried to avoid fantasizing about it.

There was also an indelible sadness and helplessness in that house.

He assigned me my first job, which was to organize his books and belongings stored in the seminary attic. Working with those materials allowed me to construct a portion of his life. I found his *Shas*, the complete edition of the Talmud with its sixty-three treatises. It was worth a small fortune. I could see all the pencil notes that Leonard, as a brilliant student, had made during his school days in those volumes. One day, I mentioned to him that I went through his books looking for his notes to help me with a text I was struggling with in class.

"Don't you have your own Shas?" he asked, between surprise and pity.

"No," I replied with the obviousness of someone living on a tight budget.

"So, you can take that one. It's probably molding anyway. It's a gift from me!"

I couldn't believe it. It took me a couple days to bring all those books from the attic to my room. And since that time, I've carried them wherever I've gone, from city to city, house to house—in every place I've lived.

"If you want, you can have lunch at my house this Saturday," he then said, after talk of the books. And, sensing a hesitation on my part: "And you can also join me at the study meeting we hold every Saturday afternoon at Sylvia Heschel's house..."

This was a meeting of some of the greatest Talmud scholars in New York, perhaps in the world. Could I, as a mere neophyte, participate in such a learning session? What a privilege! I would be in the home of Sylvia Heschel, the widow of Abraham Joshua Heschel, the most renowned Jewish philosopher of the twentieth century. I immediately accepted. It felt as if the heavenly gates of opportunity had surrendered to me!

The following Saturday, there I was at my professor's house and lunch was quiet and melancholic as usual. The passing of hours felt like an eternity—until we left for Mrs. Heschel's. This was my opportunity to be alongside the most respected teachers, and feel a part of an illustrious circle. My expectations of excitement and enthrallment soared. I wanted to tell my colleagues where I was going, and of my hope of entering very sophisticated worlds, which I knew existed around the city.

We entered an aristocratic and ancient building that faced Central Park. I believe it was at 80th Street on the Upper West Side. Mrs. Heschel welcomed us at the door and was happy to see a young student that afternoon. Every Saturday, several gentlemen-scholars met to study together. There were also a few women, but it was clear that they were either the men's wives or Mrs. Heschel's friends.

I was immediately impressed: seated around a long table were twelve—maybe fifteen—illustrious and veteran rabbis. Everyone looked at me with a mixture of joy (because my presence radically lowered the average age of the room) and a certain amount of astonishment, which could be translated as *What is he doing here?* I smiled and tried to answer the question for myself, evoking some sense of worth. They treated each other like old partners, interspersing learned anecdotes with quotes, or gently mocking each other with jokes that mixed humor and erudition.

After each half cup, the sweet Mrs. Heschel gently replenished the tea, washing all of this down. She was a pianist, and it was clear that this was not her world but a legacy of her late husband—a giant in thought and activism. Heschel was a personal friend and partner of Martin Luther King, Jr., and he had been at his side fighting against racial prejudice and the Vietnam War.

Then they turned to the page and paragraph where they'd interrupted their study the previous Saturday, and began to read and make comments. I didn't participate in previous meetings, and they read Aramaic, the Talmud's language, at a pace proper to those familiar with the text and context. In fact, I struggled to understand what they were saying, and it felt as if I was absent unless someone, lost in thought, occasionally glanced in my direction.

When someone is explaining or expressing themselves, they often look at others to gauge the reception of their words. When such a glance came my way, it took only a second for the person to see my face before realizing I couldn't understand anything; at that point, his gaze would abandon me.

The afternoon was ending, and the sun's resilient rays on that late summer day—it was September 19—illuminated parts of the table. Boredom overtook me, quickly transforming excitement into discouragement, since I hadn't participated in the discussion at all. I felt homesick and wasteful, as if this wasn't the place for me—not because I felt inadequate among the academics, but because the whole situation felt somehow insufficient. In fact, my eyes watered (not enough for a tear), and a tightness in my throat and soul suffocated me.

I tried to resist; I turned to the text or fixed my gaze on whomever was speaking. But it didn't help. I found courage but it didn't last, and soon, I gave up completely.

At some point, I mustered my courage and whispered into Rabbi Leonard's ear that I would go down and get some air at the entrance of the building or in the park. He looked at me, perplexed, as if to say, *Are you kidding?* He must have been astonished at how I was not taking advantage of the opportunity before me.

Without further explanation, I headed towards the door. I stepped out into the corridor, desperate to breathe something other than stuffy Talmudic air.

I took the elevator, and when I looked at the gate that led onto the street, saw something that looked like a scene from a movie: hundreds, no, thousands of people. They passed in front of the building and were following one another in hordes toward Central Park. These weren't ordinary people. The crowd was made up of the young, dressed in colorful adornments and clothes exuding an incredible vibe. They seemed avant-garde, more tuned to style than fashion, creating an authentic, informal atmosphere. It was the kind of group you would want to blend into hypnotically!

Leaving the mausoleum feeling of Mrs. Heschel's apartment behind, I encountered that enchanting mass. I followed the group like an apocalyptic march, but not violently; it was like we were going to heaven or something of the kind. People were joyful and radiant! I wasn't sure where it was all headed, and I didn't care. I just knew that I wanted to be there among them. The purpose of the parade was irrelevant because I knew it was for the good. The feeling was in the air, and in everyone's eyes.

So I entered Central Park with the crowd and followed a fate that was no longer personal but collective. I heard sounds from speakers, and I think that because of the pleasure of being there (and the contrast of having just left such a discouraging and inappropriate place for me), I didn't ask anyone where we were going or what was happening.

Suddenly, in the middle of the crowd, a light appeared between the trees, and I could see the Meadow, the large lawn in Central Park, totally taken. Hundreds of thousands of people were already there. Amidst that murmur of a crowd in an open place, out of nowhere there was a sepulchral silence cut by the sweetest voice possible: "Hello darkness, my old friend, I've come to talk with you again." It was Simon & Garfunkel's opening with "The Sound of Silence," the most messianic-like concert ever. It was September 19, 1981.

I sat down on the lawn and started to cry. I felt as if my soul was expanding, as if I were under the influence of some hallucinogenic drug. The potential difference between one place and another was so great that I was experiencing a spiritual decompression embolism. It was more than magical; it was so transcendent that I simply couldn't stop getting goosebumps.

As the sun went down, I felt a wind that presaged the end of summer, but my shiver was internal, visceral, and not epidermal. I slept on that lawn until 11 p.m., and only then, returned to the seminary.

I wondered what Professor Leonard and everyone else thought about my disappearance. In those pre-mobile phone days, life would continue in mystery until the next day—or longer. But I also didn't care what they thought.

On the way back, I walked the streets alone. The songs still played in my soul. I tried to explain to myself that serious and important study of cutting-edge thinkers could also be a holy responsibility.

It was clear how the sacred has its own time, embedded in the appropriate and singular existential moment. The study of the Talmud symbolized the heavens and spirituality, and the recreational and entertainment musical event, the mundane. But our souls and their role in life are unique, and in this context, the mundane could be transcendent and the metaphysical could be trivial and boring—contingent on whether our souls have or do not have a place there. The supernatural can be profane and wordly, while the holy can be mundane and irrelevant. Life and the unexpected are the keys to entering the sacred and discovering its magic.

ASTROLOGICAL POWERS

I received a call from the publishing house wanting to finalize a release date for my new book, *Fronteiras da Intelligência*. The publisher was Campus, a subsidiary of Elsevier, which focused on books with a more specialized and scholarly profile. They were beginning a new series and launching books in humanistic and even mystical areas, as was my case. I believe it was with this eagerness that the editor-in-chief informed me: "We would like to set the date for your first book signing."

I found it strange, because the author is usually the one to determine his schedule, but I agreed. He then explained: "Our publisher has hired an astrologer to inform us of the best time for launching events. We are using this strategy in coordination with our marketing sector. Do you mind?"

I asked if this was just a personal issue with the publisher, and upon hearing that it was, I agreed. What harm would there be? I found it curious that such a serious publisher had concern for astrological decisions, but it was okay by me as long as they continued to consult my schedule regarding the chosen date.

A few days later, I was informed of the date the astrologer had picked, and since it didn't conflict with any other commitments I had, we confirmed my first book signing for a bookstore in Rio de Janeiro's Rio Sul Tower. The editor told me he was also organizing an interview with the well-known journalist Marília Gabriela to be recorded in São Paulo the day before. I was happy because I was an admirer of Marlia and thought her program was very engaging.

And so it was. Since there was no possibility of meeting people other than in person, I flew to São Paulo and recorded the interview the night before the launch. This is curious: the fact that at the time there was something resembling the "virtual" which was "recording," that is, something very different from the "virtual" that we experience today. It was not virtual for the ones interacting, but it was for the public.

As expected, the questions of the interview were challenging—some even provocative—as Marília was a skilled interviewer. She was primarily interested in the book's thesis, which discussed the wisdom that can be found beyond the tension between ignorance and intelligence. To put it another way, I was writing about domains beyond the reach of logic, necessitating the richness of intuition and even premonition.

"Do you know when life points somewhere without our having the support of reason?" she asked me. This theme aligned closely with the book's concept of exploring religious mystery, albeit from a cognitive and mental perspective. Attentive to the audience, Marlia interspersed questions of a personal and theoretical nature, demonstrating a journalistic skill that admitted the concept while keeping both feet firmly on the ground.

Early the next morning, I took the first flight, arriving in Rio de Janeiro on a beautiful morning when the city was just waking up. Landing at dawn in Santos Dumont Airport evokes nostalgic sambas that touch the soul. It was very early, but I had an early appointment in Copacabana. I would have an hour, or a little more, to wander around the busy neighborhood just beginning its day.

When the first stores on Avenida Nossa Senhora de Copacabana open, they arouse my desires, excited as I am by the possibilities of purchasing and consuming. And while contemplating my dining options in Copacabana, I also recalled my son's birthday wish: a television. This was when children didn't have their own computer or phone, or both, like they do today; he dreamed of having his own television set in his room.

I entered a store specializing in household appliances, the kind that usually had all of its walls covered by televisions, all set to the same channel—a synchronization that generated an interesting effect, like those elevators with mirrors on the walls that, opposing each other, infinitely reproduce the same image. Such elevators made me anxious. I know that the intention was the opposite—to reduce the feeling of confinement, but it threw me into a hallucinogenic spiral, a kind of spatial limbo.

Now, what size television should I choose? It should be a television that is not too small to disappoint, nor should it be too large to stimulate our consumerism further, as we parents sometimes do when purchasing fancy presents for our children.

Something strange caught my attention: all the televisions synchronized in silence, like a water ballet, all showing the same scene in which the top of one of the Twin Towers in New York City was on fire. For a few moments, I wasn't alarmed because I saw the symbol of one of the major networks at the bottom of the screen, which led me to believe it was some afternoon thriller film being shown.

But wait a minute. What was going on? It was eight o'clock in the morning—time for news, not for popular science fiction films!

Hundreds of sets imprinted and reproduced a disturbing scene in mute, leaving both sellers and buyers oblivious. I went to a salesperson and asked, pointing to the televisions, "What's happening?"

"Do you like this one? Do you want to know the price?" he replied, still sleepy, starting his daily routine.

"No, I want to know what's going on!" I said, pointing to the screens.

As if coming out of a trance, he looked for a remote control and began to give sound to that eerie silence. That was when reality became even more bizarre than any fiction from an afternoon film session: a plane had crashed into the North Tower of the World Trade Center. I was stunned by what appeared to be a terrible accident. It came to my mind immediately that I had launched books at the Borders Bookstore on the first floor, there.

Borders was a gigantic three-story bookstore with a reputation for being more intellectual, despite its colossal department store-like facilities. Eventually swallowed into bankruptcy, as a result of pressures from Amazon and Barnes & Noble, the memory of being in that place came immediately to mind, including images of my son (then only four years old) running through the aisles of books, my wife chasing him, as I answered questions from avid readers. It was the práxis in New York to release books three or four weeks in advance, allowing people to read them and engage in discussions with the author, and then hopefully spread "buzz" to the rest of the country.

Little by little, people stopped in front of the wall of televisions, and then the commotion started. We began to experience altogether that time frozen in history when a second plane crashed into the South Tower. We, strangers, gazed at each other in horror, as if we had just found ourselves shipwrecked together.

People started extracting flip and foldable cell phones from their pockets, speaking rapidly into them. Suddenly, I found myself calling home. It felt like the world was about to end, and I desperately wanted to know where my wife and children were, as if a Hollywood plot was engulfing us all. News of other reported attacks compounded the sense of impending global doom. It seemed certain that a nuclear war was about to take place between the planet's powers, or that there would be an extraterrestrial invasion that would take us all to the end of time.

Once I was sure they were all okay—I don't know where I got the idea that they wouldn't be—we exchanged worries and anxieties with the people standing near us. Then my phone started ringing, as other people attempted to reach me. I interrupted a conversation to answer. It was Marília Gabriela.

"Nilton, for God's sake... what is this? How crazy!"

"Yes, crazy!" I replied, thinking she was referring to the attack, but it wasn't exactly about that.

"Nilton, what are we going to do with our interview? I can't broadcast today what we recorded yesterday! It will look as if we are lunatics. The entire planet is now talking about this, and it would look like we're talking about platitudes, as if nothing was happening. No way! I spoke with the producer, and we're thinking about calling you, recording your statements about what's happening now, and interspersing them with images from the interview we did yesterday. What do you think? Do you think you can do it?"

I agreed, and we did so. I soon remembered that if this was a problem in the case of the interview, what about the book launch, which would take place that evening? I called the editor, who was in shock.

"What a situation! It's unbelievable that we conducted such extensive consultations with the astrologer! We're going to have to fire this woman!" he said, somewhat embarrassed and indignant.

I didn't say anything, but I thought, *How strange that she chose this day among all those possible: September 11, 2001.* It was, definitively, not a favorable night to launch a book. She must have seen something in the conjunctions and quadratures of that day.

The night was a fiasco. Apart from me, some family members, and the editor, no one came to my signing. Rumors circulated that there were still unidentified flights carrying terrorists in the air. Several people told me they wouldn't go to the Rio Sul Tower because it could be a target. Everyone's gaze remained fixed on the television, replaying those scenes repeatedly, akin to a traumatized person overly recounting their experiences.

And Marlia Gabriela's program, which usually got one or two percentage points of viewers on the Ibope scale, had six points that night. She expressed her happiness and attributed it to our conversation, which intertwined the phone call about the attack with excerpts from our recorded conversation about the book, all set against the backdrop of a photo of the terrible burning buildings in New York. Perhaps they paid attention to our interview precisely because everyone was already exhausted from watching the scenes of what had been previously unimaginable.

So maybe the astrologer wasn't wrong. I was impressed. If it had been an ordinary day, with a book launch taking place like all others, the publisher's choice of date would have been—routine. And if, instead of working for a book publisher, the astrologer had played the lottery that day, or advised the U.S. Secret Service, then she could have made history.

Rav Sheshev, who was blind, sensed the Angel of Death at his side when he was in the middle of the market. He turned to the Angel and said, "Are you going to take me like this in the middle of the market as if I were an animal? Come to my house!"

Next, the Angel of Death appeared to Rav Ashi in the market. Rabbi Ashi said to him, "Give me thirty days so that I can complete my studies, as it is written: 'Happy is he who comes here [to the heavens] with his study completed!'" And when the Angel returned on the thirtieth day, Rav Ashi asked him, "What is your urgency?" The Angel of Death replied, "Rabbi Huna bar Nathan will be next right after you! And, keep in mind that the Scriptures dictate how one instance must be in close proximity to another."

TALMUD MK 28A

DANCING TO THE END OF LIFE

I felt tempted to use the real name of the protagonist of this story since many people already know what happened. But to keep my freedom in narrating the facts, I prefer to use a fictitious name.

David was a well-known businessman with many contacts in Brazil between the 1960s and 1980s. He organized parties for Brazil's powerful authorities, then under military rule, and for politicians, which were also quite renowned. These usually took place on Avenida Beira Mar, in the center of Rio de Janeiro, facing Aterro Park and Flamengo Beach, framed by Guanabara Bay and the majestic Sugarloaf Mountain in the background.

David had already retired when we first met. He was an experienced man from a traditional family of Rio's elites, and came to the synagogue in the white clothes he always wore. In this more mature phase of life, he had become spiritual; he had undergone the famous Fischer-Hoffman Process in psychoanalysis, which proposed to "kill the internal mother" and all the issues that we bring from the deepest part of our childhood into adulthood. He was now a courageous person who attended workshops that required dedication and boldness.

I knew he had also attended Siddha Yoga, an organization based on Eastern philosophies created by Swami Muktananda, now deceased. Gurumayi Chidvilasananda, the spiritual leader of a conglomerate of ashrams in India and elsewhere, led the group, which had its headquarters in South Fallsburg, New York.

Sometime in the 1990s, I was there with my family and gave a talk. The ashram is very beautiful. I was so impressed to see a building entirely dedicated to silence and stillness such that its many anterooms became increasingly imperious to sound, as the acoustic lining was more absorbent than in the previous one, making the silence ever more and more penetrating. It's curious that as the outside quiets down, our internal resonances become louder and more disturbing.

I knew David by sight. When he approached the synagogue, he was very respectful, wanting to restore his relationship with tradition. He quickly made friends and became close to the regulars. He stood out because of his white clothes, the ever-present white Panama hat, and noble air. He was a large and elegant man. It didn't take long for him to assume a certain leadership role. He was always telling stories about his spiritual adventures, whether in Siddha Yoga, the new therapy workshops he frequented, or even the spiritual sessions he had attended in Rio and Presidente Prudente, where a famous medium of the time lived.

However, what most distinguished David was that, during Saturday morning prayers, every time the liturgy reached a specific song, he began to cry. The song had a European Jewish tone, like a *niggun*—a typical Hasidic melody. His crying was not out of an emotion, but rather a catharsis. He began to sob as if a burning lava of feelings were emerging from the center of his soul. Some perceived it as a form of remorse, while others attributed it to visceral nostalgia. His father had been strict and religious; perhaps something of this had penetrated his soul, to the point of needing the Fischer-Hoffman method and others to access these depths.

He was quite a fascinating man. He was smart and had the experience of someone who had lived in the real world, acquainted with its tricks. At some point, it hit him—the urgency of some spiritual need. Many saw in this the fear of accountability—which aging brings about—before the celestial spheres, and he revealed something in this sense, as if he was in a rush to recover part of a life lived in the material and mundane sphere, in anticipation of an approaching divine audit.

I loved interacting with David's news and mischievous forays into worlds of magic and esotericism—more than, in general, I allowed myself to, or took an interest in. I found it all enriching, full of enthusiasm and openness. But not everyone's reaction was the same as mine. Reb Zalman, a very spiritual and special rabbi (whom we met earlier in the graveyard wedding), went berserk when we brought him to Brazil and he met David. I remember that during a workshop, Reb Zalman spoke to him and came away with the impression of deep spiritual entanglements in his life and history. But then, Zalman implied the need to resolve pending issues.

It seemed that David wanted to make up for something, as if he had little time and could not waste a moment of this existence doing *teshuvah*, or self-reconstruction. His contrition and anguish manifested in several situations, but nothing would compare to his weeping with that specific liturgic song. It was chilling and he made sounds that evoked poignant regrets like those portrayed in Dante's disturbing images, alarming the spirits of everyone nearby.

David would always share an experience from his week, which would captivate the group around him and encourage them to listen attentively. People avoided sharing some of these adventures with me, believing they were too "heretical," and wanting to protect the rabbi. Other times, David would appear with guests from the most distant spiritual places to learn about the synagogue service. He did this with enormous pride, always emphasizing how intensely spiritual the synagogue was. Once, he appeared with the mother of the newly elected president of Brazil. There was David, mediating between the president's mother and her brother, who had serious issues of his own.

David's desire to do something meaningful in the spiritual world tormented him. He always got involved with those who were sick or had a serious problem, either trying to mediate a spiritual cure or bringing some resources from the supernatural world to help. And it wasn't just that. I remember when, in the middle of the

Gulf War, Saddam Hussein was launching missiles at Israel, David tried to convince me that he should get on a plane and immediately go to Israel to volunteer to fight. David made it clear that he wanted to do something meaningful and make a difference. He questioned whether it wouldn't be more valuable to take a chance on a meaningful and dedicated death, than to simply succumb to death eventually by natural causes. This image of death gaining momentum after a certain age, shortening the distance, remained in my imagination.

David once came to me with an unusual worry. He told me that he had participated in a weekend workshop and, amid his meditation, had an extraordinary vision. He uneasily reported that he found himself dancing with none other than Gurumayi, the leader and guru of the Siddha Yoga group. With shining eyes, he reported: "She was beautiful and glorious! We started dancing in a circle. She took my hand and smiled at me. I felt like she was floating—it was more than a dance! It was very magical and real. I finished the meditation as if I had experienced one of those childhood dreams in which you get a gift you always dreamed of receiving and wake up fascinated."

I admit that I heard it without much surprise. After all, when we meditate, we evoke dreamlike journeys with one eye looking inward and the other outward. What David had described was, therefore, not extraordinary. But I couldn't ignore his excitement, and it registered in my memory as he related his vision. He felt overwhelmed, as if confronted with a genuine dilemma. My difficulty in sharing his astonishment came from the fact that David attributed immense meaning and value to absolutely everything—as if life were a riddle, something that only someone open to very implausible things could feel and understand.

A week or two later, during our conversation following Saturday morning services, David informed me that we would meet at a bar mitzvah ceremony I was conducting at the Great Temple, to which he had received an invitation. He was radiant then because it was a place that brought back childhood memories. The "Great Temple" is how Rio de Janeiro Jews refer to a large synagogue built in the late 1920s on Rua Tenente Possolo Street. It is not the oldest synagogue, but it's a landmark in the local Jewish community, as it represents the first post-immigration generation and their ability to present themselves with dignity. It is an important beacon, planted in the soil of the national imagination—in the center of the then-capital, as a symbol of solid and consolidated citizenship.

I occasionally conducted religious services at the Great Temple, a by-then practically abandoned location. The community had left the downtown and Praça Onze regions where they had initially settled, migrating to places like Tijuca, Flamengo, Laranjeiras, and later, Copacabana. Even so, some people still chose to conduct and attend services in that imposing building, full of memories.

And so that late afternoon was for me full of thoughts of the past. I was already worn out from having led services on Friday night, Saturday morning, and now, in the Great Temple at the end of Shabbat. And the day was yet not over! There was still a wedding to celebrate in another location, so I quickly collected my belongings and prepared to leave for this last appointment. It was at that moment when David approached me to say: "Rabbi, today is the happiest day of my life!"

Despite my task marathon, his statement caught my attention. I turned and looked at him. So he continued: "I had never been present to all the services on a Shabbat. And now I attended all the services—last night, this morning, this afternoon, and now at the closure of Shabbat—and I feel enveloped in light and serenity. I am complete, and I tell you that today is the happiest day of my life!"

I smiled, perhaps not entirely convinced of his hyperbole, classifying it as part of his use of exaggeration and drama. But I wished him a good week and hurriedly left to avoid disrupting the tradition that dictates "only the bride is late."

After the wedding, when I returned home, I had several messages waiting on my answering machine. One was from someone in David's family, who asked me to contact them, and when I did, they relayed the news: "Rabbi, David left us today."

I couldn't believe it. I had just spoken with him a couple hours earlier, and he told me that this was the happiest day of his life.

Then I was told what happened. After the ceremony, people went down to the hall, and the party began. David loved to dance and, with immense joy, joined the dance circles typical of Jewish festivals. He danced effusively with an ecstatic and deliberate smile on his face until, out of nowhere, he fell to the floor. In the dancing circle had been several doctors, including one actually holding hands with David. But David, the doctor found, was almost immediately lifeless. The smile remained on his face, but his soul had left in the middle of the dance, without a single expression of pain or agony.

Like a movie, I started replaying some of his lines, from "Rabbi, today is the happiest day of my life!" to those in which he recounted the ecstatic and rapt dance he had danced with Gurumayi. He had experienced a vision of his departure from this world, and now I could understand the awe when he told me about his premonition. I believe he understood it and was amazed at the peace it brought him. Far from terror and fear, he was shocked by the revelation—the same revelation a Hasidic rabbi once made to a disciple who begged him on his deathbed to return in a dream to tell him what it was like to die. The rabbi fulfilled the promise, saying that dying was as smooth as "pulling a hair out of a glass of milk," but that sheer fear of dying would make him not want to live again. At this point, I remembered David's tears during the liturgical hymn and his apparent sense of urgency, which we all witnessed.

I had lost a friend. In a way, he was a spiritual luminary that was near me. I knew I hadn't understood the whole process. Something, however, had become clear: when we take the reins of our destiny in our hands, deep meanings open up, and we gain spiritual powers capable of impacting our trajectory. Just as Leonard Cohen created the song, "Dance Me to the End of Love" to talk about the passionate power of generating purpose for life, spirituality can also guide, step-by-step, this dance until the end of our days, helping us not to lose the rhythm and choreography until the last moment—literally, dancing to the end of life.

TOURISM POST-MORTEM

Judith was one of our spiritual teachers. Her transformation into a Buddhist and her hospitality to all the Rinpoches—practical-minded Lamas who visited Brazil—were not the only reasons. Her life was ripe with potential for drama, which she managed to turn into an exciting journey of adventures.

She wrote a marvelous autobiography that contains incredible insights and "outsights" into the girl who had been part of the Hungarian Olympic skiing team before the Second World War and had survived the Holocaust. She joined the Resistance and had to face things like rape and the harsh reality of having to kill in order not to die. The title of her book says it all: *There Is No Problem!*

I knew her from several retreats and workshops that she attended, but she always appeared on my radar around the Jewish New Year. I had adapted a Jewish ritual to take place at sunrise, which we carried out every year on the Arpoador Rock, on Ipanema Beach, in the early morning, some years even when it was chilly and rainy. And Judith, already in her eighties, was the only one who dived into the sea at the end of the ceremony.

I bring alive, now, the memory of her figure on the rock—the body of an elderly woman who had worked out her whole life, about to jump into the freezing sea. Meanwhile, I and the others standing there, shivering and simply imagining the touch of water on her skin (not ours!). Later, with her hair wet, she would show up pleased with herself and the experience.

Her Buddhist positivism was also an important part of her character, though sometimes it seemed incompatible with the Jewish realism in which I was immersed. And our bond had another significant detail: she'd discovered that I loved skiing and that every year I went skiing somewhere in the world. Some years I even went twice—sometimes alternating between Europe and the United States, and other times, to Chile, where my aunt lived. I spent many of my holidays there. In fact, my interest in skiing originated in Chile.

With its combination of a slender silhouette and proud posture, leaning against the Andes covered in snow, Chile is an elegant country. Judith, who for years could no longer afford the luxury of a fracture or rupture of ligaments, asked me to always dedicate the first descent to her—something I did and still do to this day. The first descent is for Judith, and it's often the last nightcap too! Connecting with someone who had mastered the sport and was intimately familiar with the cold and altitudes evoked a sense of tradition and a nostalgic memory of the icy-silent landscape.

Every once in a while, she would appear at the synagogue after one of her trips. She'd traveled the whole world, and this was not just a way of speaking; she wanted to know the planet from which she had germinated and sprouted, and refused to leave without paying homage to it and getting to know its anatomy. It reminds me of the beautiful story of a rabbi who lived near the Alps, and once, amid his studies, looked out the window and saw those great mountains in the distance. He closed his book and said, "Creator of the universe, I am here to study the sacred texts, but I must know Your work and pay my respect to Your creation"—and promptly left to explore parts of the world he didn't know.

I admit, however, that I was curious to know where the funds for her extensive trips came from. I knew they were austere trips; she loved being close to the people and their culture; and she was a frugal tourist. But the fact is that since the 1960s, she had been a secretary to senior executives. I believe she provided herself with some war compensation. Or, perhaps, she gave herself the right to visit her world, and that kind of boldness often takes people very far.

One day, Judith called me early in the morning: "Nilton, I want to tell you something I won't share with many people." From her perspective, there was always good, or at least stimulating, news. I imagined she was going to or returning from a small country that I'd never heard of, tucked away in an exotic part of the world. "I have cancer," she went on, "and I refuse to undergo treatment. I've already decided that I don't want to submit myself to medicine and its outlook on life."

This shocked me, so I researched the situation to determine its gravity. The situation was dire. Unfortunately, it was at a palliative stage and all that remained was to try and extend her life. She explained that she would enter unknown territory with no return and would not delegate sovereignty over her life to science. "Science and knowledge could not—and perhaps would never—understand life," she explained to me.

"I've decided to pursue my own life rather than trust doctors who can't cure me. I choose to embrace life, as it consistently offers a remedy. But I wanted you to know. I might require assistance with my son or face other potential situations, and I kindly request that you honor my wishes."

I immediately agreed to be a partner or midwife in this process, already imagining what the world would be like without Judith.

After this, we communicated more frequently. Sometimes I wouldn't speak to her for two or three weeks, but we always found a way to connect, and she kept me informed about her issues, especially about the pain she was feeling. Fighting pain is an inglorious thing because it robs us of all the resources we need to face it. Pain contracts and retracts, making it challenging for the soul to stretch, leading to its gradual stiffening. However, she was brave and would take this dispute to the limit.

Her Buddhist athlete behavior reminded me of jokes about the tough gauchos from my hometown in the south of Brazil who, despite suffering, maintained a defiant smile even while a tear slowly formed in the corner of their eyes.

She always started by saying that everything was great, and little by little I got to know the details of her reality, interpreted and mediated by a powerful faith. Her disease's consuming audacity advanced like a tide that brooks no objection.

In the meantime, I received a visit from a desperate mother who had discovered a serious illness in her teenage daughter. She was my son's friend, and the doctors suspected a rare and extremely aggressive form of cancer. Although the mother was visibly in panic because of the disease, it was the implicit nature of her angst that deeply affected me. The prospect of not only death but also sequelae and limitations, particularly in young people, deeply affected me. I attempted to soothe them while simultaneously striving to calm myself. This double struggle to calm others and yourself most of the time does not end successfully. How is it possible not to identify with someone if you have children of a similar age? I remember a rabbi who, upon seeing a breathless woman from afar carrying an injured child, shouted to help her: "Calm down, calm down!" But as she approached and revealed that the child was his grandson, the rabbi's tone and content changed to, "My God... my God... help... help, fast!"

Instead of words of consolation, a comforting attitude was required. Judith's name and the title of her book appeared like an apparition before my eyes.

Then I explained the situation to the terrified mother and daughter who were waiting for help: "I can only think of one person to call in a situation like this!"

"Who?"—they both jumped out of the chair in a gesture of hope.

"Judith."

I put myself on the task of convincing them Judith was a master in the art of *there is no problem!* I believed that telling them details about her condition, that she was seriously ill, and her fearless way of living, would convince them. Or perhaps it was the genuine scarcity of alternatives that convinced them.

They were so excited that I immediately came to my senses, reminding myself that I had to arrange things with the other side first. What would Judith's reaction be once she was overcome by pain and engulfed by the confining that disease imposes? How would she react? Would she have the courage to help at a time when she needed so much? The most common thought in pain is *I don't care*, and I wasn't sure how she would embrace the prophetic exuberance I said that she possessed.

I told the mother and daughter that I would speak to Judith and get back to them. Then I called Judith. She didn't answer at first, but I persisted until she finally picked up the phone. She began talking frantically. She said she was facing a big challenge with the pain. I empathized with her for a few moments, but at the first opportunity, I brought up the subject of the young woman. "Judith, I have a situation that, in my opinion, only you can handle."

Suddenly, her voice rose in pitch, akin to an intravenous injection of enthusiasm. I didn't need to explain much, and not only did she agree, but she asked me, for obvious reasons, to hurry. She set a condition, however: that they call the day they would visit, to check if it was a good moment to come. Her reaction pleased me, particularly because she didn't ask for details of what was being expected of her.

I wasn't sure what she should or could do. I felt a tinge of uncertainty, considering that it might not have been true intuition, but rather an insecurity stemming from the deep effect it had on me leading to dumping it in her lap. Things like this happen, and we unconsciously delegate and evade.

Within a few days, the meeting took place, and the result was far beyond what I had imagined. The young woman's mother called to thank me. She said that Judith was a "great little witch"; that the visit had done everyone good; that they left feeling light and confident; that everything would work out; and that "There is no problem."

I was overjoyed. It had worked.

But I soon contained my joy, and the hint of pride that I held for my intuition in making a good choice when thinking about Judith, disappeared. If the girl's illness worsened, it would render our efforts futile. How far can we confront the monster with the simple assertion that the problem doesn't exist? It seemed that it would only be non-existent, subjugated by Judith's belief, as long as it didn't have a major impact on the young woman's life. I clung to the fact that Judith was in such a defining phase of her own life that, to support this statement with faith, something special and magical she intuited was about to happen.

I was even more astonished when, after a couple of weeks, the mother called again. "Rabbi, my daughter is cured!"

"How?"

"She underwent new tests, completely ruling out the horrible diagnosis they'd given her. What she has is much less serious, and with a simple surgery, everything will be fine without any risk."

She thanked me and said that every year, on the exact day of the meeting with Dona Judith, she would go with her daughter to the synagogue to have an *aliyah*, a blessing next to the Torah. To this day, they still follow this way of giving thanks.

Judith was thrilled with the news. They even visited her a few times—with Judith now as the girl's adoptive grandmother.

A few weeks later, Judith died. She managed to stay at home and was not hospitalized. She resisted the temptation to avoid her encounter with this aspect of life, and descended her final mountain. I imagine she did so exultantly, with the cold wind making her cheeks red and gradually restoring her youth and flexibility for the final descent, full of joy. Her zigzag in this last snow is now without a trace—just a path, without a past.

I was mistaken. Not much time had elapsed, and her son told me that Dona Judith had prepared ten travel packages before she died. Together with her travel agent, she left an inheritance of ten trips planned for ten very dear people in her life, each with a companion. She associated each of her ten favorite places on Earth with their personalities. I wasn't among them, because she took care to give gifts to people who never had the financial means to undertake trips such as these: her manicurist, her maid, a nurse, a friend—in short, people who received a ticket, destination, accommodation, and cash for their respective adventures.

Judith was wise! Not only did she know how to magnetize materials with immaterial value, but she knew how to extract the "last one" for herself from all of this. This was one of those pranks that God, with a smile on his face from one side to the other of the universe, embraced. She was the one who initiated the concept of post-mortem traveling and post-mortem tourism. And just as she went down with me, on my skis, on each first descent of the slopes, she was also in the luggage of the hearts of those ten people and their companions, honoring the beautiful world that God gave us.

A typical skier's jocularity comes to mind: "Just one more time, one more descent... will you?!"

Rabbi Hanina said: “The demon Jonathan told me that spirits do have a shadow, but that it doesn’t move like a human shadow!”

TALMUD YEV 112A

PENDING ISSUES FROM THE OTHER WORLD

This next story weaves together events from my dear master Reb Zalman Schachter-Shalomi's first visit to Brazil. Reb Zalman was the founder of the Renewal Movement in Judaism, a type of neo-Hasidism. What made Zalman such a special personality, in addition to his charisma and sensitivity, was the combination in him of the traditional and the avant-garde, the orthodox and the liberal.

Born in Ukraine, Reb Zalman survived the Holocaust by fleeing to the United States early in his religious formation. The Chabad Movement in New York adopted him, and he emerged as the "golden boy" of the Lubavitch Rebbe, spearheading a dynasty that would significantly impact post-war Judaism. The Rebbe summoned him and Shlomo Carlebach, who would later become a prominent figure in twentieth-century Jewish music, for a special mission, recognizing them as among their most insightful and innovative students. In the mid-1950s, the Rebbe realized that it would be necessary to improve the dissemination of Judaism to new generations, and he gave the task to these two bright disciples, Zalman and Shlomo. The goal was to infiltrate the academic environment and influence the young at North American colleges and universities to become involved with the tradition.

The result was exceptional, and, like everything that is out of the ordinary, determining whether it went in the supposedly right (expected) or wrong (unexpected) direction is a matter of focus and point of view. Indeed, both individuals made significant contributions to the new generation, yet their surroundings also shaped them. Shlomo became the most important singer and composer in American Judaism, winning the hearts of an entire generation through his passion for music. Reb Zalman, in turn, took a more intellectual and mystical path. In the university environment, he became acquainted with other religious traditions, marveling at the spiritual diversity of the world and its manifestations. He became a professor of comparative religion and was familiar with the effervescence of the world in the late 1950s and 1960s. His spiritual audacity led him to interact with various traditions, including the original American peoples, Buddhism, and Sufism, from which he gained the title of sheikh, further adding to his eclectic formation.

To get an idea of his spiritual boldness, we can mention the fact that Reb Zalman joined psychologist and neuroscientist Timothy Leary—an icon of the 1960s—to study the therapeutic and spiritual benefits of LSD in his experiments at Columbia University. Zalman served as a volunteer in the "experiment tanks," where scientists tested psychedelic adventures.

When I met him, he was already a legendary character. I was in Israel one April for Passover when I found out he was taking a group of people to celebrate the feast at the top of Mount Sinai, in the Sinai Desert. We met there, forging a special connection.

Upon receiving my rabbinic ordination and returning to Brazil, I nurtured the aspiration to introduce him to the tropics. There was something Brazilian about Zalman: perhaps his multifaceted persona, or his flexibility and sense of inclusion—traits that we usually identify as Brazilian. Many of these characteristics of Brazilianness are fanciful when contrasted with Brazil's social reality. However, I believed that there was something worthwhile in the amalgamation and aggregation of our culture that would make his visit have a great impact on the way Jews understood their tradition. And Zalman's approach to tradition of looking forward rather than simply in the rearview mirror, seemed profoundly auspicious to me.

To attract him to my proposal, I talked a lot about the magic of Brazil. He knew about the richness of Afro-descendant traditions and the shamanic culture which existed there. He had also heard a legendary story about the rabbi and philosopher Abraham Joshua Heschel, from when he visited Brazil. He was Sylvia's husband, about whom I wrote in the story about Central Park. According to the myth, Heschel came to Rio de Janeiro in the early sixties at the invitation of Rabbi Lemle, an important leader of that generation. Heschel asked Rabbi Lemle to take him to see Brazilian religious manifestations, and so he took him to a Candomblé temple. As soon as Heschel entered the room, the priest, the *babalorixá* who had already incorporated one of the deities, stopped the drumming and said in a voice from another world, "Someone has entered here who is greater than me." And, according to legend, he called Rabbi Heschel to the center of the yard and asked if he could pass energy around.

I am pretty sure it was curiosity about Brazil's spiritual life that convinced Reb Zalman to ultimately make the trip.

I devoted myself to planning several events that would fit his schedule. He would only be able to come in December, during the days that included Christmas and the New Year. I imagined doing a miniature "Woodstock," not only because of the avant-garde atmosphere and informality, but also because of his youthful conviction resembling a kind of revolution.

I convinced the synagogue where I worked—the only non-Orthodox one in Rio de Janeiro—to bring Reb Zalman and hold the events that I was planning. Despite its liberal religious stance, the synagogue was quite conservative, a typical trait of the culture of Germanic immigrants, informally known as *yekes*. A yeke is a kind of nerd: a meticulous and rigid person, but intellectually open, although in the field of behavior and flexibility things are always different. In any case, the synagogue's president and the senior rabbi agreed to the undertaking, as long as I would raise the necessary funds to carry out the project. To this day, I don't know if I convinced them with the argument of attracting a young audience, or if they didn't take me seriously, certain that I wouldn't collect the required amount anyway.

I scheduled an interview with a big businessman, who welcomed me despite being very busy and somewhat impatient. Between him taking one phone call and another to interrupt our conversation, he turned to me with an air of *Who is this guy anyway, and what does he want from me?* I must have initiated the presentation several times, but as the phone kept ringing, he paid little attention to what I said.

Until suddenly he replied, "Rabbi, I've been through a difficult time, but thank God things are better now." And then we started talking about a difficult period in the man's life. That was the moment, during a pause in our conversation, when the two of us become more intimate. After this, he asked, "Now, what is it that you expect from me?"

"You know, the event, the arrival of the rabbi I told you about..."

"Oh yes, of course. One moment." And he picked up the phone and called his events director, who entered the room within seconds. He gave him instructions to help me in any way possible. He assured him that I would organize a large-scale event and should receive all the necessary support.

The event was going to take place, and now I had professional coverage as if I were holding a commercial event. I could print leaflets—something that was done at the time for publicity purposes—and I could count on the infrastructure I wanted to put that "Woodstock" into practice. This encompassed a fully equipped circus tent to accommodate the events, portable restrooms, and many other innovative ideas. And so it was underway.

A campground was our setting, and we provided all the amenities of a large rock concert, including accommodations for approximately two hundred-and-fifty people and a large camping space that could accommodate up to a thousand more. The surprising thing was that the event took place at Christmas, which, despite being an available date for Jews, competed with the summer and the end-of-year atmosphere—a time when no one usually commits themselves to anything that might conflict with family gatherings. Even more surprised was the synagogue management when registration was full, since they hadn't believed there would be any demand whatsoever!

Now Reb Zalman was a *rebbe*, a specific designation in Jewish tradition that symbolizes mystical leadership, but not in the esoteric or magical sense of the term. A rebbe has the gift of sewing together worlds, of looking at a person's exterior and x-raying their soul, like a tailor capable of sewing together body and soul, outside and inside. The imaginary, the collective unconscious, the atavistic, and the ancestral entwine with a person's internal world, making it separate from this world. While the world here is a place of awakened and conscious people, the other world is a dreamlike place of synchronicities, archetypes, and symbolism. A rebbe even has the talent for facial recognition of someone's human spirit, seeing beyond their countenance.

Stories from the past recount rebbes who could read thoughts on a person's forehead, and anecdotes suggest that many, apprehensive of their thoughts' exposure, attempted to conceal their faces with hats. Of course, the trick didn't work.

Reb Zalman personally met with individuals and x-rayed their spirits, delivering the report to the patient in real-time. Some had ordinary burdens, originating from their particular lives; others, in more serious situations, had connections and entanglements with other people—or, even more sensitively, with previous generations and their family's past. He buried the unfinished business, or the pending issues, deep in the viscera of those he attended. Akin to the spiritual practices we employ in Brazil to treat physical ailments, these unresolved issues focused solely on spiritual healing of the spirit and providing "psycho-subtractive" remedies from the spirit, which serve as countermeasures against somatization and physical manifestations of psychic disorders.

Reb Zalman's ability to make visible links between the psyche and physicality impressed everyone during his visit. And, of course, when it goes beyond parapsychism, things get even more interesting. People get emotional when they see the capillaries that connect their symbolic world—or their ancestry, their archetypal designs, and their synchronicities—to the real world of physical experience.

One of these experiences occurred during a speech he gave in the event's central space, taking place at the circus tent. The plenary sessions and main celebrations were held in an open field on a farm in the Sacra Familia municipality. At one point, a woman stood up and made a statement. "Rabbi, my mother passed away last year, and she is not at peace! I know she's not at peace... How do I know that? Because strange things are happening in the house where she lived, like disturbing sounds heard throughout the premises, events of items breaking or moving out of place, and we don't know what to do."

Reb Zalman invited her to move closer and posed the following question: "What's your mother's name?"

"Rachel," she answered.

"In Hebrew?"

She spoke her mother's name.

Then Zalman looked up toward the ceiling, or the heavens, and cried out, "*Ruchale!*" This is an affectionate diminutive in the Yiddish language, equivalent to "Little Rachel." It was a way of invoking and beseeching her appearance. His tone of voice was a perfect combination of intimacy and summons.

At that moment, out of nowhere, a terrifying wind blew over the circus tent. It was December 25, in the countryside of Rio de

Janeiro, around eleven-thirty in the morning. The day was beautiful; the blue sky was cloudless and clear. There was a bonanza—those lulls typical of the summer heat around noon. But suddenly it became dark, and random and unexpected gusts almost tore off the canvas roof. All the ropes and stakes tensed, producing an even more frightening sound. Surprised and ruffled, people got up from their chairs in an instinctive reaction ready to flee. Some people even ran from the tent.

At first, Reb Zalman seemed surprised himself by what happened, but then, gaining composure, he resumed: "*Ruchale, tiere ruchale*" [Little Rachel, dear little Rachel!] he exclaimed, before continuing, "*Was tut sich bei einem im Boich?*" ["What's wrong with your stomach?"]

In Yiddish, this expression serves as a direct demand akin to, "Let's stop playing games"—an invitation to maturity and objectivity—while simultaneously questioning what was so indigestible to Rachel, a person whose memory was blessed.

Immediately then, the wind stopped. People looked at each other, and amidst the buzz of comments, they sat down again.

Reb Zalman then stopped speaking as if he were directly addressing Rachel. Turning to her daughter, he told her that whatever was bothering her mother, we would say a *kaddish* for her at that moment, that is, a prayer for the peace of the deceased, adding that the daughter should make a charitable donation in the name of her mother, Rachel. He then proceeded with the prayer. Finally, he concluded by telling the daughter that she should repeat the prayer to seal any remaining debt on the coming Holiday of Yom Kippur (the Day of Atonement).

Something surprising happened in that episode: It felt as if we had witnessed a conversation between a living person and a deceased one. Nonetheless, it was done with a respectful mystery that kept the conversation from becoming inappropriate or overly explicit. Therefore, the hidden remained camouflaged and preserved, without necessitating further exposure beyond its existing state.

While he was in Brazil, several people reported similar experiences in which Reb Zalman unearthed something hidden—although latent—within themselves and, in doing so, helped them recover a liberating wholeness.

These were unforgettable events for those who participated. It was as if my rebbe had validated a new form of attention or sensitivity, and the participants returned home, impacted by new subtleties. Some of them even had the bonus of settling or cancelling old and ancient debts.

TELEPATHIC CONVERSATIONS

The retreat with Reb Zalman was cathartic. At that time, at the end of the 1980s, there was a substantial interest among the general public, as well as the Jewish community, in spirituality generally. I was about to deliver the manuscripts for my trilogy on Kabbalah, which would become a publishing success in Brazil. This was the same time period and publishing house during which and where the yet unknown Paulo Coelho was publishing his book, *The Alchemist*. There was a real sense of interest in these subjects!

That may explain why Zalman received so much attention from the Brazilian media. At the end of the year, the media space opened up for the enigmatic and mystical. From the cover of *Manchete* magazine to several headlines in the *Jornal do Brasil* newspaper, Zalman's presence became bigger than the events we planned, and certainly bigger than our synagogue.

I remember one famous journalist receiving an assignment to interview Reb Zalman. His name was Fernando Gabeira, and when he first arrived at the interview, he showed little interest, as if you could tell he was writing an article simply to fill space in his paper at the end of the year. Little by little, however, Gabeira became enchanted by this New Age character as he questioned Zalman, who in turn closed his eyes and after some silence returned as if he were waking up from a journey inside himself.

I remember Gabeira asking, not without a hint of provocation: "Reb Zalman... why did you just close your eyes before answering my question? Was this style intended to evoke the aura of a spiritual guru?"

"No, no way!" Zalman replied in surprise. "These interviews tend to have very similar questions. I close my eyes to ask myself, *What was your response the last time you faced that question?* Then I ask myself again, *How would you answer that question today, at this moment?* This pause helps us realize how much we have moved through life and what transformations we have been going through."

I'd planned two more big events: one at Circo Voador, open to the public, and another at the synagogue, which would take place on December 29. The synagogue management summoned me to express their concern regarding the importance that Reb Zalman's presence had taken on. They asked me to stop the interviews and halt the dissemination outside the Jewish community. I tried to argue that this was all to the good, but they were unconvinced.

Another issue arose when I ordered the production of thousands of flyers, each featuring an illustration of a person wearing Jewish religious objects such as the skullcap and tallit, the mantle, and traditional prayers. Furthermore, he appeared to be in the lotus position, or *asana*, a specific sitting position in yoga with legs crossed. These leaflets greatly disturbed the city's Jewish Orthodox wing, which decided to hire an advertising agency to counter the wave that had taken over Rio de Janeiro. In a curious and long document, all the city's Orthodox rabbis (including many who did not get along well with each other) unanimously signed an ad in a newspaper that said, "Judaism is like a mother; you only have one!" Taking advantage of the festival of *Hanukkah*, which recalls an episode in which Jews overcame the temptation to become Hellenized or assimilate to the invading culture, they accused our synagogue of leading young people astray. And, under pressure, the synagogue leadership asked me again to suspend any interviews or exposure to the media.

I ended up surrendering, and, already thrilled with the retreat and all its repercussions, I agreed to discontinue any form of divulgation of this kind.

In the meantime, Reb Zalman urged me to teach him more

about Brazilian spiritual life, and Rio specifically. I was then the president of ISER, the Institute of Religious Studies, which paved the way for Viva Rio, an NGO that would support innovative projects in deprived areas of Rio. Because of this position, I contacted Mãe (Mother) Beata de Iemanjá. She was the priestess of an important candomblé house, or *terreiro*, in Nova Iguaçu, leading hundreds of thousands of faithful of African origin in the Baixada Fluminense suburbs of Rio. I arranged for Zalman and his wife, Eve, to meet Mãe Beata, knowing that her shamanism would appeal strongly to him.

Since I was completely involved in organizing the event that would take place that afternoon at Circo Voador, I asked Rubem César Fernandes, an important anthropologist and executive secretary of ISER, to accompany Zalman, Eve, and Mãe Beata while they were together. So that Zalman and Mãe Beata could communicate satisfactorily, Rubem—a person with enough sensitivity to appreciate and mediate such a meeting—would act as an interpreter, a job he gladly accepted. I warned Rubem not to disclose anything about this meeting to the media. The atmosphere in the synagogue was tense, and I wanted to avoid further controversy. Since Rubem was committed to this, I could relax and devote myself to organizing the events.

I later heard news of the sublime meeting that took place. Rubem told me that he was a completely expendable character, as there was no need for an interpreter.

Since it was the end of December, there was torrential rain in Rio de Janeiro, late in the afternoon. A storm, filled with thunder and lightning, engulfed them. Upon entering the *terreiro*, the temple, in the middle of the storm, as soon as Reb Zalman and Mãe Beata became aware of each other's presence, a loud clap of thunder shook the place. Mãe Beata exclaimed in ecstasy, "The rabbi is from Exu!" With that thunder, the orixá of communication and language started the meeting.

Rubem told me that Reb Zalman, out of respect upon entering the temple, removed his broad, colorful skullcap and offered a large, captivating smile. He said that from then on, they communicated without any difficulty: gestures, expressions, smiles, movements with hands over the heart, hugs, and touches made talking unnecessary. It was a magical meeting of two souls, according to Rubem, accompanied by lots of rain and the fragrance of humidity mixed with the heated concrete, and the plants in the garden.

Mãe Beata blessed Reb Zalman, and then asked him to bless her. He did so in total communion, as if they were old friends who knew each other's world and traditions in detail. Deeply moved, Reuben shared his thoughts with me: "What I saw today was telepathy! I had never witnessed an act of communication in this sphere. It was more of a harmony than a language. Empathy is more than comprehension."

Several thinkers, including Freud, Lacan, and Derrida, have discussed "telepathy" as a realm beyond the dichotomy of "knowledge/non-knowledge." This is due to the common traits and characteristics of beings of the same nature, which turn language into a pleonasm, a repetition of previously expressed ideas. Rubem, as an anthropologist, was fascinated by the experience and remarked that traditions are languages or codes, allowing wise people of different traditions to communicate through correlations in their traditions and experiences. I was enchanted by it all, but I barely had time to listen: that night we held the event at Circo Voador.

As I introduced Reb Zalman at the beginning of the proceedings, I realized that he was neither a singer nor an actor, and that, beyond the language barrier, what exactly was he going to do or perform?

His presentation that night was similar to his encounter with Mãe Beata earlier in the day. Once again, I'd planned for translation, but Zalman spoke mostly through music, jokes, facial gestures, and sounds. It was unlike any lecture; the primary focus was on the form, rather than the content, of the speech.

The following morning, when I arrived at the synagogue, the doorman said to me, “They are in a meeting, and they’re waiting for you!” In a meeting?! It was the end of December, and there had been no board meeting scheduled. But as I entered the boardroom, there was the senior rabbi, the president of the synagogue, and some of the other board memebers. The president approached me with a newspaper in his hand and said, “What is this?”

“What do you mean?” I replied, genuinely perplexed.

Then I looked down on the board room table in front of me. I was shocked to see there, printed in large letters on the newspaper *O Dia*’s front page, “AXÉ RABBI!” next to a large photograph of Reb Zalman blessing Mãe Beata with his hands on her head.

I’d been strongly warned against anything ending up in the media. I had expressly asked for this not to happen.

Everyone looked at me with suspicion, and maybe disgust. It was undeniably on the front page of Rio’s most popular newspaper. But how? *O Dia*’s audience was primarily from the humblest classes, and their paper was extremely popular. Its circulation exceeded that of the next two most important newspapers in Rio de Janeiro combined.

Once the initial impact waved over me, I struggled to control my astonishment. Then, a positive feeling set in, and I couldn’t contain myself. “Gentlemen,” I said, “I swear, I don’t know how this happened. I recommended everyone be as discreet as possible, and I canceled several requests for interviews.”

The looks on their faces said that they were unconvinced. I went on. “However, look at the positive side!”

Everyone looked at me as if I were a lunatic.

“What an incredible opportunity! A rabbi blessed the spiritual leader of hundreds of thousands of people of African origin,

Umbanda and Candomblé! For us, Jews, who are always seen as extraterrestrial and hermetic, having this beautiful image—of a priestess asking for a blessing—is very positive. It is powerful! For Jews, generally seen as a distant elite, this is an incredible opportunity to move away from the stereotype!"

But clearly, I wasn't convincing. They warned me again that this would be the last time, and that I would have to be even more careful going forward. The synagogue itself would officially host Reb Zalman's final scheduled performance the following evening.

When I left the boardroom, I called Rubem César and asked if he'd seen the paper. Did he know what happened. He told me: "Oh, sorry, I forgot to tell you about that. When we arrived, I was informed that Mãe Beata had invited a reporter from *O Dia* to document the meeting. Mãe Beata said that people are trying to destroy her work, and evangelical Christians are attempting to convert *terreiros* into evangelical churches. She wanted a record of her African-based tradition side-by-side with another Western religion."

With the mystery solved, I went to the newsstand and bought several more copies of that day's *O Dia* to keep as souvenirs. And to this day, the scope of telepathy is fascinating to me. In Greek, *tele* means "far," while *patia* means "passage": the distance approached via a path or a way. That telepathic coming together of distinct and distant traditions was worth all the publicity embarrassment felt by my board!

Anyone who enters a city and fears the evil eye must hold his left thumb in his right hand and his right thumb in his left hand and say, "I, so-and-so, am a descendant of Joseph, upon whom the evil eye has no power!"

TALMUD BER 55B

MESSIANIC TIMES FOR A DAY

The final event of Reb Zalman's visit was a talk at the synagogue, with content focused on the Jewish community. I believed it could be a turning point and an opportunity to renew our faith.

It was the penultimate day of the year—a time when it is not customary to hold events. In fact, the synagogue wanted to give its employees time off, but we had this event already scheduled.

Like the Woodstock Festival, no one expected an audience. However, given all the controversies (and publicity!) around Reb Zalman's presence thus far in Rio, and since the rabbis of the more Orthodox wing had shown strong vocal opposition, it seemed that everyone who was anyone wanted to be there. Rumors circulated that more radical groups might attempt to disrupt the event, but all that mattered to me was that the tickets had sold out, with over two thousand people registered and many more on a waiting list.

The night before the synagogue event, I fulfilled a promise to Reb Zalman by taking him to witness a candomblé ritual near Irajá. He enjoyed it intensely and respectfully, taking an interest in the details of the liturgy and worship. We left after midnight, with me worrying at the wheel because it was a very violent period in Rio. That Saturday night, there were shootings, and at the time, we didn't have apps that announced where they were taking place.

I was speeding along the empty streets when Zalman asked, "What is this?" I hadn't realized it, but we had just passed a large iron gate inlaid with the Jewish symbol for the Star of David. At first, I didn't even recognize it, but I quickly realized that we were in Inhaúma, in front of the Polish Jewish cemetery.

This story, if not paranormal, is certainly out of the ordinary.

At the beginning of the twentieth century—and for almost a hundred years—Polish Jewish women prostituted themselves in cities such as Rio de Janeiro, São Paulo, Buenos Aires, and even New York. Born in Eastern Europe and known as Poles, these prostitutes were poor, often illiterate, and without a dowry for a good marriage. Many fled their countries, threatened by waves of antisemitism, and ended up being recruited by pimps, many of whom were also Jews.

I tried to give Zalman a brief overview of this. He was fascinated that this was the first exclusively Jewish cemetery to open in Rio. They established their own sacred space because of their stigmatization and inability to be buried in the Caju cemetery, which had a Jewish section. Thus, they preserved their traditions and maintained Jewish rituals. They also paid a cantor to officiate at the High Holidays, as they were not welcome in the city's synagogues.

He said, "Let's stop!"

I tried to convince him that that was a dangerous idea. But he insisted, saying that nothing would happen to us and that we could not leave without saying kaddish—the prayer for the dead—for those women. I had no choice but to pull the car over.

We got out and I looked worriedly in all directions. Reb Zalman, in turn, went to the gate and looked into the Polish cemetery in the early hours of a Rio de Janeiro morning, not long before the sunrise. I had to surrender to the moment, which was in fact serene and very touching. There was Zalman, saying the prayer in a perfect sober tone, and Rio's pre-dawn responding with an unusual peace, including the crow of a nearby rooster, and, in the distance, the faint music of a samba circle.

The following day, I took Reb Zalman and his wife Eve out on the town again. As I knew of his interest in the "fruits of the earth"—what he called emanations and manifestations of our planet, reflecting parts of the world in its unique fauna, flora, fruits, and cultures—I prepared a basket with the most exotic fruits of tropical Brazil: soursops, cajás, custard fruits, cashews, and several types of mango. We engaged in conversation around each of these fruits new to Zalman. And he recited the *Shehecheyanu*, a specific blessing in the Jewish tradition for situations in which we experience something new or unusual. We spent the afternoon this way until I took them to that final synagogue talk.

When we arrived, the synagogue was completely packed. I was ecstatic, feeling that something enormous and important was taking place. I noticed familiar faces and thought, I'm glad so and so came. It's going to be incredible!

I felt a sense of joy when I realized that everyone who was supposed to be there seemed to be present. It was a unique opportunity. Even the identifiable presence of some Orthodox religious people who were there to criticize or interfere added to the sense that something exceptional was about to happen. Reb Zalman was planning to talk about a new way of looking at the world. And seeing and hearing him on that occasion, with his deep knowledge of tradition added to his creativity and charisma, I knew it was going to be glorious!

With great aplomb, I went to the microphone and briefly announced his entrance. When Reb Zalman took the stage, a dense silence of respect and expectation ensued. Then he made a brief introduction, and before he even started warming up the night with his ideas and concepts, he said, "I will take three questions from the audience!"

I awakened as if from a trance. What? He was already announcing the end of something that hadn't even begun? I didn't understand what was happening, so I ran to the stage through a more discreet entrance on the side. I went up to him on-stage and whispered in his ear. "Reb Zalman, we have as much time as you want... Spend an hour or more, and then proceed with the questions. Keep going."

Embarrassed, he turned to me and said: "The fruits..."

"What's wrong with the fruits?" I asked as if it were an esoteric riddle.

"The fruits have given me intestinal problems. That's what's happened." All of this we whispered back-and-forth, as a captive audience watched us in silence.

What a concrete and blunt reality this was. It was an elementary and obvious thing, but it also didn't make sense. This is not how the evening was supposed to go! How could we lose this spiritual opportunity because of something so dramatically physical and mundane?

And, of course, reality imposed itself: Reb Zalman answered the three questions, which were disjointed from each other because he had not yet even presented much of anything for them to consider. He responded to each questioner with his typical elegance and wisdom, but the conversation didn't gain momentum. Nor could it. Zalman thanked them, and people began to get up to leave—as Zalman made a rather quick exit.

I'm sure the audience wasn't as disappointed as I was, as they didn't know exactly what to expect. I could have explained that Reb Zalman wasn't feeling well, but I complied with his request to simply withdraw. I suppose he could have made an excuse to save face, but he chose not to. I was devastated.

Some people from the crowd passed me and said, "Very nice!" but I couldn't judge whether they were trying to be kind, or whether, from their perspective, what he had said was genuinely interesting. I didn't think that was likely.

As I went to the parking lot to find my car at the end of the night, people consistently halted me voicing their praise for the event, acknowledging the numerous consecutive events we had organized with Reb Zalman in Rio, or simply to engage in brief conversation. This happened also when Zalman's driver pulled up alongside me. A window opened, and Zalman emerged from it.

"Sorry, dear Nilton... I know you expected more. A lot more.

However, that's how it is... It's not possible to do certain things in one night. You have many years of work ahead of you. Most people lack this openness and energy, which, though intense, remains diffuse and lacks the power you envision."

Then the window closed, and the car drove away.

This warning was ringing in my head. I vaguely understood that the attempt to lead people to certain truth or awareness does not happen simply by convincing them. Some walls are very resistant, and a period of erosion is necessary for them to give way. Furthermore, the deconstruction of paradigms is a prerequisite for the emergence of new ones.

My youthful spirituality aged a little that night. There are things on the threshold between heaven and earth that are impossible to manifest. I realized that messianic utopias, standards revolutions, or simple maturity cannot be rushed. Moses believed the path was more important than the arrival because he focused on the process done in the desert. The tropical fruits, innocently, marked the end and limit of the fleeting flavor of messianic times.

EXCLUDED FROM PARADISE

My situation at the synagogue became stranger after Reb Zalman's visit. It was a combination of me seeming like an *enfant terrible*, that is, an indomitable spirit full of ideas (and putting them into practice), and of the very success of the venture itself. Success always changes an environment and requires maturity of everyone involved to understand the transformation that's taking place. I could sense a peculiar atmosphere growing, and endeavored to avoid further actions that might be construed as potential offenses.

Early in the morning on the day after the talk at the synagogue, I went to the flat where Reb Zalman and his wife Eve had stayed. It was one of those huge apartments on Avenida Atlântica facing the sea that someone had lent them. A renowned master's visit to the city created opportunities for the wealthy, who are always needy in the spiritual realm. Someone had generously offered us the apartment, along with a driver and a cook, who greatly assisted me in arranging food and transportation for our two guests.

One of the most effective ways to assess a person's virtues and vices is to observe their relationships with those who work with or for them. Zalman and Eve excelled in this aspect. Even with the language barrier, the maid and driver liked the couple. More than liking them, these workers seemed almost devoted to our guests, as if they were aware of some real spiritual dimension in their lives.

I inferred this, while Reb Zalman and Eve were in the apartment, by observing the extraordinary concern that the driver and cook showed for them, as if they were devoted to clerics of their own religious traditions. They had even greater deference toward them than I did, which says a lot about Zalman and Eve.

When I arrived, they were packing their bags because they were leaving the following day. I'd obtained first class tickets for them, but I had to accept that they would leave on December 31. It was high season in the city, and only on that night were return tickets available.

This was a problem, because I knew that Reb Zalman would be interested in seeing the beautiful religious event that was New Year's Eve in Rio de Janeiro. Instead of the heat and smoke from traditional fireworks, which is the focus of end-of-year festivities nowadays in Rio and nearly everywhere else in the world, the heat and smoke in Rio at that time came from the dances, pipes, and bonfires of the Umbanda and Candomblé circles that took over the waterfront. I wanted Zalman to know a little more of the taste of the "fruits of the earth" in this impressive demonstration of faith and tradition.

Since their plane was leaving late at night, I knew I would be able to show my guests the beginning of the celebration before taking them to the airport. So I went to the kitchen to talk to the cook about the arrangements for the end of their stay, and I found her decorating a small wooden boat on the sink. She was making an offering to Iemanjá, the female orixá deity known as the "mother of fish" and honored at the turn of the year. "Are you ready to present your offering to Iemanjá?" I asked her casually.

"Not mine! This is for the Rabbi! He was the one who asked me to prepare it." And she pointed to the flowers, cachaça rum, and other items typical of an offering to Iemanjá, ensuring everything was as it should be.

I smiled awkwardly and went back to the room where Reb Zalman and Eve were packing their bags. I was furious. What did this mean, an offering that the Rabbi should make? Copacabana was a neighborhood with a large Jewish population, and Reb

Zalman had become a very well-known character there, both through the internal buzz of the community and his exposure to the media. This would not go unnoticed. There was a significant likelihood that people would witness him making this offer, and I was already put on notice. To put it mildly, I felt responsible, and I was concerned.

To your eyes, it may seem now like there was nothing wrong with this situation—or the proposed offering. But due to the controversies, and especially the way the synagogue was absorbing the pressure these problems were exerting, such a gesture, if made publicly, would help to disparage and discredit Reb Zalman's reputation and, consequently, mine.

At that time in Brazil, it was acceptable to participate in religious dialogue and interreligious tolerance, but this was something else entirely. This involved making a personal offering and directly participating in someone else's ritual. My mind was suddenly filled with doubts. Had I become too enchanted and brought a charlatan, one of those opportunists that abound out there disguised as healers and curers with no commitment to ancestry or the criteria of a tradition? I entered the bedroom to question Reb Zalman.

"What does the offering you asked the cook to make, mean?" I said abruptly, surprising myself with my degree of heat.

He looked at me in surprise, and before he spoke, and before I could say anything else, Eve walked into the room. She looked at Zalman in a very intimate, reprimanding way, the way that only couples or partners know how to do.

She said, "I told you, Zalman, that this is very delicate and could put Nilton in a difficult situation."

He absorbed the blow, much like a child denied the opportunity to indulge in a delectable meal or pursue a desire. He appeared to maintain his composure. And, with Eve's support, I quickly calmed down. Eve and Zalman had a mutually respectful relationship, and it was not uncommon for Zalman, despite his leadership role, to publicly turn to her and ask for advice. This was one of those beneficial pieces of advice for him to listen to, I thought.

The discomfort quietly passed, and I waited in the apartment for them to finish packing. We had an intriguing program that morning: Reb Zalman was going hang gliding! Since I was grateful he'd accepted my invitation to come to such a marginal and peripheral part of the world, I'd also planned some events that I imagined he'd never forget. Among these was the possibility of seeing Rio from above, in the silence and lightness of a hang glider. I knew that his soul would appreciate the unusual and radical nature of the invitation and that he would know how to place it in the necessary spiritual context.

A trustworthy friend of mine was also one of the most experienced flight instructors, and to him I would trust Reb Zalman's safety without hesitation. Ruy Marra was willing to take on a seventy-one-year-old rabbi heavier than air, but with a spirit as light as a feather, to soar with him over Rio's mountains, forest, and sea. While Zalman, who had eleven children, would ignore for a day that clause in his life insurance that warned against lifestyle choices deemed as excessively radical.

Zalman would later write about this flight, describing it as "a bird's dream." All non-winged species suffer from a lack of movement in three dimensions. As we transition from a horizontal plane to a vertical one, we experience a cathartic shift, breaking free from our inherited limitations and achieving transcendence. This day of flight crowned Zalman's magical visit to Brazil.

That evening, I went back to the apartment again to pick up Zalman and Eve, ready for the real flight—their return by plane to the United States. As agreed, we were going to go down to Copacabana Beach, watch the African-based rituals that took place on New Year's Eve, before heading to the airport.

The three of us entered the elevator, and before the door closed completely the cook abruptly opened it again in order to breathlessly and triumphantly exclaim: "You almost forgot it!" She reached out to Reb Zalman, and in her hands was the boat offering, fully decorated by hand.

There was a momentary, total silence between us all. I glanced at Eve as Zalman, unworried by any look on my face, took the boat from the cook's hands with a smile. Then the door of the elevator closed and the silence continued—Zalman with his conspicuous boat, and me trying to contain my indignation. We left the building, and I followed a little further behind, thinking of how I could harmonize everything with what I was feeling.

I went ahead and escorted them to the beach, demonstrating some of the ritual circles that echoed the rhythm of the drums. As always, there were many pleasant as well as nauseating odors, a lot of smoke, and discordant sounds. Reb Zalman had left the boat on the sand, and I thought to myself that there was no way I was going to accompany him when he performed his ritual.

At one point, I noticed that he and Eve had disappeared together. They'd apparently gone somewhere to perform their ritual while I remained motionless and rapt, contemplating the ceremony we were engulfed by. But when I realized what was happening, I felt very curious. How would he perform this devotional act, which was so distant from his own tradition? This was not a mere act of appreciation for something that belonged to another culture, but rather, a personal manifestation. Also, I had never seen it done before; my only relationship with this ritual, and others kin to it, was one of distance and respect.

I began searching for the two of them among the crowd at the sea's edge. In the far distance, I finally recognized Reb Zalman, who had rolled up his long pants and was walking into the sea.

A feeling suddenly overwhelmed me, telling me not to look, fearing it would be a misguided intrusion on my part. Perhaps something personal was happening, and my judgment was off.

I remembered the story of Pardes, one of the four wise men who entered the orchard. In Hebrew, *pardes* means orchard, hence the etymology of the English word "paradise." Pardes is also the acronym for four levels of interpretation according to Jewish tradition: the literal, the allusive, the symbolic, and the secret. This founding myth of the mystical schools of Judaism says that of the four wise men who entered this orchard, only one was left unharmed. As for the rest, one went mad, another became a heretic, and the last one died.

Territories are not spaces, but instances. Entering them may seem wrong to those in other spheres, to the point of losing reason, faith, or life. Understanding modifies reality, so I had no access to the place into which Reb Zalman entered. I could try to force my way in, but I would see and experience everything in a place from which I could not leave unscathed.

It would be several years before I was able to talk to Reb Zalman about that night and that moment beside the sea in Rio in the hours before his flight to return home. I told him that I had kept my distance because I couldn't follow him. Smiling, he replied that to make that journey, one must dive very deep. He also said that spiritual traditions are diverse, so they need their own form. In the depths, however, they meet and merge into something universal. If you are not in these depths, what you will see will be heretical, hallucinating, or destructive.

I don't know how his boat sailed through the waves of Copacabana. I know that Reb Zalman returned, then, to the States. As for me, I received notification of my dismissal from the synagogue a few weeks later. It was carried out in a very elegant, hushed way, and without just cause. No one would admit that I was being ushered out unjustly—the board simply explained that a different kind of rabbi was needed.

My destiny then advanced. Years later, Reb Zalman revealed to me that both he and Eve had been deeply concerned and undivided. They didn't want to hurt me professionally, but they had a strong feeling that everything had a purpose and that the seed should find better soil.

I did not enter paradise that day, and there was still a long way to go. But now, instead of following a horizontal plane's linearity, I could do so through true three-dimensional flights. I learned that you fly not only upwards, but also towards yourself, within yourself, and deeper!

"And God made the beasts of the earth after their kind!" (Gen. 1:25) According to Rabbi Judah, this refers to demons. The Creator created their souls, but when he was about to create a body for them on the sixth day, the sanctity of Shabbat began, and he created them no more!

GEN. RABA 7:5

THE FREAK IN THE MADHOUSE

On a routine afternoon, my secretary came into my office to check my schedule. As she was leaving, she suddenly turned back and said, "I almost forgot! They called from the Instituto Pinel, inviting us to participate in an ecumenical ceremony. I believe it is to celebrate the foundation's one hundred-and-fiftieth anniversary."

I had accepted that invitation months earlier. Often, the feeling that an event will occur far in the future leads me to think of it as a distant milestone, as far away as the eye can see. Until suddenly this future is on top of me, unavoidable, and a hindrance.

I now had to be at the Instituto Philippe Pinel—called the Institute of Neurology today—at 10:30 a.m. the following day in Botafogo.

That morning, after further procrastination, I was running late. I needed to get to the Rio de Janeiro Federal University Campus, close to the district of Urca, but with the traffic and whatever else had happened, I was already an hour behind. In situations like these, I usually call, make some excuses, and cancel my participation. This time, however, I couldn't find the number of the person responsible, and I decided not to break the appointment. I was sure that the event would already be over, but at least I would appear and show that I tried.

Parking in the area was difficult. But I was familiar with the Pinel building, which has its entrance on Rua Venceslau Brás, almost in front of the Botafogo Club headquarters. From there, I managed to find the auditorium where the event was being held.

I didn't realize until I was upon it that the entrance to the auditorium faced Avenida Pasteur, and that the place I was about to enter was the Emperor Pedro II Lunatic Asylum, renamed the Neurosyphilis Institute in 1937, which then became the Philippe Pinel Institute (honoring one of the first psychiatrists in history), and finally the Neurology Institute, affiliated with the Federal University.

"Pinel" has, ever since my childhood, been the politically incorrect way to jokingly call someone crazy. "Are you pinel?" Of course, this expression came to mind when I entered the building.

Once inside, I couldn't find the auditorium, and I became even more anxious as I was now ninety minutes late. Lab coat-clad professionals appeared everywhere; family chairs lined the corridors; and I was trying to find my appointment. After navigating several corridors, I breathlessly questioned two men who approached: "Do you know where the ecumenical ceremony hall is?"

Only then did I pause to take in the details of the scene: on one side, two nurses, resembling those who straitjacket patients; on the other, me, in my suit and with my hair disheveled, completely confused in the Pinel corridors.

"Who are you?" asked one of them suspiciously.

"I'm the rabbi," I replied, confident in myself.

Suddenly, I realized the risk I was taking: for a fleeting moment, I, lacking the rabbinic physique du rôle (due to my lack of a beard, the stereotypes of the Orthodox Jew, or my jovial and informal demeanor), could see his reaction to my declaration, "I am the rabbi" as if they were about to respond, "And I'm Napoleon!" I think I very narrowly avoided becoming an inmate in the Pinel.

To ease the sudden tension, I quickly composed myself and presented real data, such as the event that was taking place, the one hundred-and-fifty years of the institution, and other things I knew about where I was and what I was supposed to be doing there.

When I finally freed myself from the nurses, I learned that the event was taking place in a nearby university building, rather than at the Pinel itself. And once I made it there, at the door, the director and two other women were waiting for me. Surely the event was already over by then.

"Rabbi! What a blessing you have arrived!" they said almost in unison, with immense relief.

Their warm reception surprised me, since I was expecting, at the very least, some ironic joke or friendly reprimand for my absurd delay. "I'm sorry I'm late," I stammered. "It's just that..."

"No problem! No problem! The important thing is that you've arrived. You see, the priest and the pastor ended up canceling, and at the last minute the Mãe de Santo from Candomblé and the spiritist were also unable to attend! And we have the entire institution waiting for them."

They then pulled back a heavy and ancient curtain, revealing an auditorium that must have contained five hundred people, all sitting still in the deepest silence.

"Rabbi, they are so excited. We were afraid that no one would make it. And thank God, you showed up. Therefore, feel free to begin, and start the ecumenical service, as soon as you are situated. We're all ready!"

For someone who believed the event would have already concluded, and imagined making an excuse and returning to his life and affairs, this all seemed like a nightmare.

"What does 'start the ecumenical service' mean?" I asked, looking at them, perplexed. "Ecumenical services assume that other religions participate. I cannot, alone, do an ecumenical service!"

They looked back at me with astonishment of their own, and then, with expressions that seemed to indicate there was no alternative. If was as if they were suggesting, in the world of madness there is no such thing as impossibility. And before any other argument could occur to me, I saw again the waiting audience, looking as if they were waiting for the messiah himself. There was no choice.

I walked onto the stage and people stood up. Breaking what must have been a despondent silence in which they'd sat for so long, they woke up with sounds of applause. I quickly contemplated that I would need to enter a trance or summon an ecumenical entity in order to rise to this challenge. Perhaps I could conjure a combination of religious service and popular TV program, emulating both the popular evangelical routines and the style of celebrity priests of our time.

I began chanting a niggun, one of those Hasidic melodies consisting solely of words like "oi, oi, oi" and "la, la, la." And to my enormous surprise, I had never seen—and perhaps will never see again—such a participatory audience, as everyone, without exception, joined in. Some tried to accompany me in singing in their tones and notes, without thinking of the quality of their musical performance, but with lots of melodic feeling. Other people clapped with a smile, showing that it was a soulful act rather than a mechanical one. Still others danced or swayed to the melody and its prayer, seemingly moved by what was happening. There was not a single alienated or alien soul in that large group. We were one whole.

I recited psalms, and dozens of people moved their lips as if they were reciting a universal "amen" along with me. We were close to the end of the year, and I talked about Christmas. The simplicity of that audience captivated me, even though I hardly remember what I said. I began to realize that madness, perhaps, need not be a delusional version of ourselves or an incontinent anomaly of being, but rather something all its own.

Our consciousness usually contracts us, limiting us to a claustrophobic definition of who we are. Usually, the possibility of not inhabiting your being translates into a nightmare, an existential phobia. This was different. This was better. From a world of dysfunction came interactivity, serenity, and communion that we do not usually see on the streets or in institutional relationships.

I once met a "crazy person" at the doorsteps of the Assembly of Councilors of Rio de Janeiro proclaiming that that house was filled with "lunatics." As soon as I entered that Assembly and saw the behavior of the councilors, the concept of madness and sanity blurred before me.

On that day in the Pinel, I was a priest, a saint, a pastor, an imam, and a rabbi. Perhaps that was one of the times I distanced myself the most from myself and my identity. Perhaps I "went mad"! Who knows, maybe I was Napoleon, and even a rabbi. Hopefully, the nurses were not listening!

I understand our worries about mental disorders, and I know all about schizophrenia and possession, but perhaps we should broaden our fears to self-possession as well. Sometimes, we can find a spirit, a lost soul, within aspects of our personality that embody it. We can also perceive a tremendous amount of "craziness" coming from the outside world, specifically pointing to where our inner craziness resides. Psychoanalysis, psychiatry, neuroscience, and other forms of knowledge dedicate themselves to the exorcism of this very self-possession.

POSSESSION I: THE BRIDE

This story is filled with madness, I assure you. My commitment to only reporting things that happened remains. I didn't personally experience what I am about to share, but a close friend who frequented the synagogue relayed it to me. The story so impressed me that I used it for other purposes in a book about Jewish problem-solving, published in Brazil in the nineties, which then appeared in English as *Yiddishe Kop: Creative Problem Solving in Jewish Learning, Lore and Humor*. I repeat it here, set now in that liminal place between sanity and madness, and between the real and imaginary.

"I'm here, I'm alive, because of this story. It's no small feat!" my friend told me, after saying the *kiddush*, the blessing over wine that then turns into a celebratory snack that synagogues offer after religious services.

He told me that one time, on the eve of a wedding, a terrible growl sounded in the backyard of the bride's house in the Polish village where his father was born. Then the bride's screaming struck terror into the hearts of everyone within earshot. After all, Jewish tradition believes that a bride is vulnerable on the eve of her wedding. It is therefore customary to hold a vigil the night before, to prevent evil spirits—or evil things, in particular, including thoughts—from taking advantage of her.

Jewish folklore recounts numerous tales of brides succumbing to possession on the eve of a wedding. It is possible that the origin of this belief comes from the fact that brides were usually very young women, almost girls, and for this reason, crises and outbreaks occur as the nuptials approach. The brutality of having to leave your parents' home and live with a husband with whom you have had little or no coexistence or intimacy may explain the phenomenon.

The sound of terrifying screams coming from a bride's house on the eve of her wedding brought family and friends running to her aid—and brought cries for the local rabbi to come to the house to help unravel the mystery.

But the rabbi wouldn't come. The growls and screaming so frightened him that he decided it was too dangerous. He sent for the local fool (the "village idiot") to go and see what was happening.

So the people brought the idiot to the house and sent him in the direction from which the terrifying noises were still coming in the backyard. Before long, he returned, seemingly unconcerned. Everyone surrounded the fool, anxious and curious to know what it was about. He calmly explained that there was nothing to fear and told everyone that the frightning sounds could easily be explained: an old tree had fallen and its trunk was on the ground. Over time, the trunk rotted and became hollow, and now the wind was passing through it, producing the strange sounds.

Everyone was relieved, everyone, that is, except the rabbi.

That night, the rabbi gathered the community together and recommended that they all pack their bags; they would all leave as soon as possible in collective emigration. For the rabbi, the reason for this was obvious. And although his advice was not understood, it was received by the townspeople with acceptance.

This is the tale of a small village whose residents, at their rabbi's suggestion, emigrated, completely escaping the Nazi insanity that would soon arrive there. The rabbi had heard very real screams—screams that came from the future—and, defying the most fertile and malignant imaginations, was able to predict impending horror. The screams were therefore real. But how could the rabbi recognize all of this, given the information he had?

He successfully deciphered a riddle. The first piece of

information was the sound of a scream in a bride's house on the eve of her wedding. The madman then enters the scene, providing a rational and convincing interpretation of a natural phenomenon. Still, the rabbi is suspicious. The rabbi's order to bring in the fool stemmed from the rabbi's willingness to embrace a hidden reality, should he encounter one. Rather than presenting an absurd report that blended fantasy and superstition, the fool spoke in a manner uncommon for a madman, who does not see reality as it is. The rabbi concluded that there was an inversion—not a natural phenomenon, but rather premonitory sounds.

For the man who told me the story, the rabbi made a decision that saved his father and his entire family from the Nazi Holocaust.

I find this story very rich, not only because of its value in the field of interpretation, but because it locates the liminal place in which we live. Understanding that the supernatural and natural intertwine like alternating vibrations is crucial. Everything is natural until it ceases to be, and becomes supernatural, and vice-versa.

The bride serves as the medium, allowing the natural and supernatural to blend. The line between real and personal is discovered in that liminal zone we most often ignore. And then we are all mediums, given that we all have an identity, a bride-like vulnerability, and if we pay due attention, this will help us enter the supernatural world. And also return from it.

Abaye said, "My master advised me not to sit near sewers because demons usually haunt these places."

On one occasion, porters brought a barrel of wine and placed it on the ground next to a drainpipe. The barrel burst. Then they went to Mar bar Rabbi Ashi, who brought ram's horns (shofarot) and exorcised the creature that had appeared. Mar bar Rabbi Ashi asked, "Why did you do this?" The demon replied, "And what was I supposed to do if they had thrown the barrel at my ear?" Mar bar Rabbi Ashi responded, "What are you doing in a place where so many people are present? Since you broke the rule by being in a place that isn't yours, go and reimburse the porters!" The demon replied, "Set a time, and I will return with their payment!" We agreed on an opportune moment, but when it arrived, the demon did not appear. When he did return, Mar Bar Rabi Ashi asked him, "Why didn't you show up at the time we agreed?" The demon concluded: "We have no right to take anything that is tied, sealed, measured, or counted. So, I had to wait until I found money that didn't have an owner; here it is!"

TALMUD HULIN 105A

POSSESSION II: THE DYBBUK

In the folklore of Eastern European Jewish communities, a *dybbuk* is a human spirit that, as a result of its past sins, wanders incessantly until it finds refuge in the body of some living person, taking possession of it. The word dybbuk has a Hebrew root and means to stick or cling; in other words, it is an unsettled spirit. Shlomo Ansky, a folklorist and playwright, ignited international interest in dybbuks with his 1916 Yiddish play, *Der Dybbuk*, a classic that underwent translation into several languages.

The filmmaker and playwright Domingos de Oliveira once revealed to me that he'd made a version of *The Dybbuk* in Portuguese. I was curious and asked to read it. In addition to his work in the arts, Domingos was a brilliant thinker who managed, without altering the original text too much, to give the story a modern touch, and a very clever metaphorical dimension.

I told him, "Domingos! I want you to perform your dybbuk in the synagogue. Let's do it."

He was always involved in a thousand projects at once, and this would be yet another. However, the idea of staging the play in a synagogue made his eyes light up. He must have been curious how the occult might find resonance in such a setting. I'm sure his creative spirit got irreversibly hooked. He began to ponder the idea.

When Domingos started to imagine the cast, and when he suggested that Priscila, his wife, take part, she objected. "No way! If you want to do it, go on. But I have a strong dislike for mystical entities, including spirits of any kind. I get very tense... In no way do I want to take part in this!"

The possibility of performing a horror play within a spiritual space repelled Priscila in the same proportion to how it excited Domingos. But although she wanted nothing to do with it, she didn't oppose Domingos' request to open their house for readings and subsequent rehearsals.

On our first meeting day, Priscila distributed copies of the script to participants for a reading, and we congregated around a coffee table surrounded by sofas and armchairs. Priscila greeted the assembled cast of seven or eight, offering refreshments and engaging in conversation with all of us. Her interest was visible, and she seemed to want to participate, but her fears—or perhaps, her beliefs—did not allow her to embrace the idea.

We had barely started that first reading when a gigantic crystal chandelier hanging over the coffee table fell with a terrific crash. A combination of the noise of the impact, the smashing of glass on glass, and Priscila's scream, made us all jump from our chairs in terror. Then there was silence. We were frozen and stupefied. Until Priscila, tiptoeing quickly out of the room, murmured, "I told you... I told you not to play with these things. They exist!"

We stood there, our eyes meeting as we tried to pick up the pieces. Of course, it was all simply a coincidence. By chance, the chandelier had fallen at the exact moment we were meeting. We, as humans, are the ones who conjecture about a simple physical phenomenon like this, whereas the weight of a chandelier sometimes simply surpasses the resistance of its screws.

We thought about all this, even verbalizing some, with reasoning that straddled the line between rationalization and pure denial. The choice, which implies intentionality, is consistently more confusing. A second possibility is to transform the world into a continuum of purposes, finding reasons for great absurdities. This is always a human dilemma. And perhaps it is the dybbuk itself—the intellectual haunt that the supernatural imposes on us.

Our intellect is flexible, and if we guide it to receive certain information, it will extend into implications that encompass all the other ideas or concepts we have, like a spoonful of sugar in a jug of water. Trying to keep the information contained in a single part of the intellect without communication with everything else is the definition of superstition—from the Latin *superstitio*, which means "prophecy" or "excessive fear of the gods."

The future and fear are the powerful nutrients from which our imagination conjures superstitions. To a certain degree, we all harbor remnants of information that we persistently conceal to prevent them from influencing our more objective thinking.

In the legends of the dybbuk, human concern with issues beyond life is always present.

Only humans can create this fear of not carrying out or correctly exercising their life's purpose or function. And the idea that we leave debts in this world is probably the central reason for the existence of ghosts. Unfulfilled expectations and dreams turn into mourning spirits, devastated by their loss. As a result, these spirits are toxic byproducts of regret. I'm not talking about skepticism, but the need to know the contaminations and side effects that impact human thought and imagination, as well as how to make allowances and approaches.

On that day, we overcame the heavens' warning, continued to read and rehearse our performance, and eventually we proceeded with the event in the synagogue, situated in the penumbra and enveloped in shadows. That foray beyond imagination was extremely beautiful, and there is no doubt that the atmosphere of the space that received it contained nuances and angles for talking about the afterlife.

For some inexplicable reason, the fact that everything proceeded without any sinister complications reinforced my sense that something extraordinary had taken place. Because what cannot be known manifests itself through synchronizations and signs, but also concealment, as everything ghostly is more powerful as a silhouette and an absence than as a materialization.

Domingos often told me that he was an atheist or agnostic. I understand that intellectuals and artists often make this choice, or find themselves in such a place. However, I had already noticed his fascination with the "beyond," with the possibility that there is something outside the borders that mock and demoralize normality. The natural world derives beauty from its realism, but it can also be dull and oversimplistic—too normal and excessively objective.

A SEMI-IDENTIFIABLE OBJECT

I'm unsure whether I should talk about this at all. What will people think of a rabbi who has seen flying saucers? Yes, I know... Or rather, yes, I know, people are dubious about unidentified flying objects.

I'm not sure why I'm apologizing so much: if we can't identify them, this is merely from our lack of understanding. I am interested because flying saucers imply both the existence of "internal entities" and extraplanetary bodies. Let me explain...

The encounter took place when I had just taken time off from my university course to volunteer on a kibbutz, something very appropriate to both aspects of my identity at that time: Jewish and young. My work at the kibbutz was the dignified job of garbage collector, with noble tasks that included piloting a small tractor that pulled a skip on its trailer. I am confident that my vessel would have been visible from space. After work, I used the same tractor to collect kitchen trash and other waste. Then began a fantastic journey: I passed fish farms until I reached the beach, and from there, along the deserted sand, I traveled ten kilometers with my "residual ship" until I found a landfill that was about five hundred meters from the coast.

Every day I repeated the same work and route, as content as I could be. Some of the unforgettable memories of freedom and emotion in my life at that time were the solitude of that ritual, shared only with Pink Floyd, and the song "Echoes," which I never tired of. I crossed that terrain as if I were entering a new territory—a fresh configuration of time and space dictated by my infinite youthful future.

I keep trying to recall how I listened to those songs, but neither the equipment nor the technology that allowed me to repeatedly listen to a cassette tape, already damaged by overuse, comes to mind. Though I believe it was a tape recorder, a vague memory of something magical contradicts that.

Every day at sunset, exactly at the time I chose to carry out my trash responsibilities, I heard an iconic transmission that could only come from a radio: "From somewhere in the Mediterranean, we are The Voice of Peace on 1540 kilohertz... and as the sun sets..." It was *La Voix de la Paix*, a radio station offshore that, for twenty years, broadcast in the Middle East from a former Dutch freighter, MV Peace, anchored off the Israeli coast. I found myself in my vessel while The Voice of Peace navigated its vessel, evoking the sensation that the entire world was steering itself in one direction or another.

But this day wasn't like any other: I was young and lived in a community with other young volunteers. At such an age, everything social has an astronomical dimension and importance. I excelled in my advanced Hebrew class and successfully passed the exams to gain admission to the Technion, the most prestigious technological university in Israel. However, I missed my family and life in Brazil, and I had decided not to continue with those plans. In fact, that day, during language class, the teacher asked each of us about our plans, and I talked about my situation.

Because our past lives transport us to a location that differs from the actual place where our experiences took place, I can't pinpoint precisely what transpired next. It's similar to clicking on the little yellow man on Google Maps to view a specific location. Despite technology's ability to rotate the image three hundred-and-sixty degrees, we perceive a significant reduction in focus and scope. And besides, memories fade. I do remember, however, that people were extremely critical and negative regarding my decision. Somehow, the combination of social pressure and a personal issue, maybe it was my latent insecurity, had left me deeply shaken.

Without anyone noticing, I held back tears, which only came when I left the classroom. I couldn't say why I was so upset. Do you know exactly when you're going to freak out? Hardly ever. When it seems like there's no way to counteract a feeling that's forming like a massive wave that's about to swallow you whole, when it seems like you won't have enough breath to emerge triumphant from the other side after diving in and overcoming it—that's how I felt that late afternoon as I took my trash ship to undertake another sanitary mission.

I was weeping and listening to my music along the same route as always, like a ritual. Then suddenly, still in daylight, I could see an object approaching, flying some thirty to forty meters from the coast on a trajectory parallel to the beach. There was no one around. I stopped the tractor and got out, walking towards the seashore to observe it more closely and precisely.

This strange object, covered in flames, approached with enormous speed. I tried to fit it into a traditional pattern. Was it an airplane? Or was it a meteor? Or, in a region rife with armed conflicts, could it have been some sort of missile? Something was happening, and it was important.

I looked around again and realized I was still alone. But looking back on the hillside of the kibbutz, I saw a figure. The object then followed its trajectory and passed right by me. And at that moment, I finally saw it most clearly: it had a spherical tip and a flame at the back—like a comet. It didn't look like anything I'd ever seen before, and it was close enough for me to make sure it wasn't on a downward trajectory, which is what you'd expect from a meteor.

And so it went its way, leaving my imagination on fire. Astonished, I started talking to myself: "What the hell was that?"

Next, an inexplicable euphoria overcame me. Seeing the improbable or supernatural is empowering. I'm not sure if this is because of the knowledge we've gained, or the sense of expanding our horizons—allowing us to expect much more. I sped to the dump and disposed of the trash almost carelessly, anxious to go back and talk to someone about what had happened. Thousands, or perhaps hundreds of thousands, of people live in that region. After all, it appeared to be heading toward populated cities, so of course everyone would be talking about it!

I returned to the kibbutz immediately after my work was done, when people were already at home. But I couldn't find anyone. The first person I came across was a friend, who, surprised, told me he hadn't seen anything. His lack of interest made me quickly look for another witness. I passed a colleague who had been in the class I had left earlier, feeling so upset. At first, I avoided her because she was one of the most unpleasant people that day. Her name was Sidsil, a name that I associate with a witch from a folktale. However, I was so curious and excited that I found courage and went to talk to her. I stopped the tractor and asked if she'd seen anything strange near the beach.

"No—but it is funny, now, that you asked, because I remember seeing you on your tractor in the distance, and yes, there was something. I don't know why I didn't pay much attention. I just registered that it was you and something in the sky, without much interest."

With a delicate smile on her face, she expressed her interest in understanding why my classmates' questions had shaken me so much in class, rather than focusing on unidentified flying objects. She was enigmatic, and her attitude caused me to think of class events as overlapping with afternoon events from another planet. This brought me back to the feelings that had preceded the apparition. I had forgotten and set aside my small earthly problems for a while, focusing on discovering the improbable and unfathomable.

Sadness immediately returned. And Sidsil, I thought to myself, with her equivocal but amiable appearance, really did look like a witch. Nothing in the cosmos possesses the existential power of the little things in our lives to disturb, or shake us up, restoring us to a sense of reality.

So I had found no witnesses. On the other hand, I knew I wasn't having delusions. As emotional as I was, I had taken no drugs, smoked nothing, and was in full possession of my senses; and, as transcendent as the experience was, the smells of garbage and the garbage collector accompanied me. I finally went to the shower to see if it would wake me up.

The following day, the friend I'd questioned came to tell me the news he had read in the newspaper about something strange appearing in the skies the day before. That's still all I know about my flying saucer from sources outside of myself.

Today, I think I must have seen a meteor. I watched videos of rocks from space entering Earth's atmosphere, and yes, they somewhat resembled my unidentified object. However, mysteriously, what I saw in those films was different, as those boulders were falling to Earth rather than taking the long horizontal path that I witnessed.

This leads me to another theory of what happened all those years ago. Perhaps young people at the beginning of their adult lives live in parallel universes. They are on the edge of establishing contact with the alien version of themselves, while immersed in a world of choices and definitions. At this stage of life, over a period of a few years, we transform into completely different people, unrecognizable from our previous selves, and there may be a chance for a meeting.

I miss my tractor. The world's waste and garbage lay behind me, while the shore's border framed the horizon ahead. Could the unidentified future, then, be that object?

I was shocked when, a few weeks after returning to Brazil, in the same area where I was making my daily trips in Israel, a terrorist attack occurred. Extremists boarded a boat and disembarked right there, killing a journalist who was taking photos. I thought that I too could easily have had such an encounter. Some things on Earth are more amazing and terrifying than those in heaven.

ELVES AND SALVATION

The first job I had on that Israeli kibbutz, before becoming a garbage collector, was in a plastics factory. The factory offered volunteers the opportunity to work through the night, and only three nights a week, instead of five days if you had the day shift. I thought it was a bargain, and for a while, I went through the experience of a night shift worker.

The strangest thing for those who work under these conditions is not so much the issue of exchanging day for night, but living against everyone else's schedule, for better or for worse. Without a doubt, it was wonderful to see the sunrise and have the freedom to spend the entire day free. In addition, I remember enjoying the best breakfast possible, since coming home at the end of hard work, I was hungrier than ever. However, night workers also experience a sense of loneliness, as our availability doesn't align with others.

In an attempt to cope with the sadness of the situation, I saw on the kibbutz bulletin board that there would be a trip to the Sinai desert with a group of Norwegian volunteers. This was during the time when Israel had not yet returned the Sinai Peninsula, occupied in the 1967 war, to the Egyptian government. I had several days of vacation time accumulated, and saw this as an opportunity.

The Norwegians were a closed group, perhaps because of the language difference, and they tended to socialized only with one another. I have to admit, however, that many of the women fit the beauty standards of the time. They were European, mostly blonde, and made up the majority of the group. I was glad that I signed up to go.

On the day before the trip was to take place, something strange happened. The work at the plastics factory was quite repetitive, involving the production of round containers used for chicken feeding throughout Israel. The machines required periodic collection, stacking, and replenishment with fresh plastic grains. And every time a machine presented a problem, we had to turn it off, wait for it to cool down, and then turn it back on. This led to some tense situations, and the manager was adept at making people feel awful about the losses in productivity that happened as a result.

That night, during my shift, I was very tired. The hours were not passing quickly, as they usually did, and the machine was opening and incessantly spitting out more and more of those red things to feed the chickens. There is nothing worse than defying the rhythm of machines and relying on your tempo. I was fighting sleep, and my head dropped down with an embarrassing frequency. I was desperate, and in that state between waking and sleeping, I thought it wouldn't be long before I made a serious mistake. And there were still many hours to go!

Then, as in a children's story, late at night, perhaps it was two in the morning, a group of children entered the factory. A beautiful teacher stood before my machine, guiding it. Nobody explained to me what was happening. My expectation was that a guided tour had been planned, but it wasn't that. Then, since the children in the kibbutz all slept together during the week, separated from their parents, I imagined it was some kind of educational project. Whatever it was supposed to be, the children kept me company, and I explained to them how each stage of production worked. The teacher's presence also would have been enough to save me from deep boredom and routine monotony. But the children were particularly cute. They were like angels or elves, filling the chilly environment with its unbearable noises with tenderness and grace, ultimately saving me from utter boredom during that night's shift.

The teacher then asked, "What's on the other side?"

I looked surprised and repeated, "On the other side?" The

distraction was enough to make my machine choke. I ran to the control panel and immediately turned it off, trying to solve the mess I had gotten myself into. When I came to myself, the teacher and the children had left.

The next day, I questioned several people about who those children had been. What class were they from? Nobody understood what I was talking about. There was no record of a school visit at two in the morning. Something was wrong; it had been too real to be a mere dream or delusion.

But then the day for the trip to Sinai with the Norwegians had also arrived. In the dawn darkness, we got into a rented bus and left. It was very early, and everyone went silently to their seats to try to take a nap during the long journey. Since I didn't know anyone, and since at that time of the morning the most I could get from anyone was a shy smile, I sat in the front seat close to the driver. About twenty women and five men made up the group. They were all Norwegians but me.

We continued to our first destination, Nuweiba Beach. The driver announced in English that we were approaching. In an act of joy, people began to take off their clothes—not exactly taking off their shirts or getting ready for the beach—but literally, they were getting naked. The driver glanced in the rearview mirror before turning to face me. I believe he realized I didn't belong to the group and looked at me to gauge my reaction.

It was as if I was being asked to accept this as something normal, but it seemed a bit bold to me to see those exaggeratedly white bodies contrasting with the dark seats on the bus. Also, I hadn't realized that Nuweiba was a nudist beach, nor that in northern European culture it was common to associate beaches with nudity.

The driver and I were now part of a subgroup. There was a difference, however: he was driving and therefore performed a role that allowed him to be a kind of authorized voyeur. The group included me, and I would soon be the only one clothed.

In my condition, I felt utterly alone. I don't know how prudish I am, but the thought of doing that just to fit in with the group bothered me. Being honest with nudity is not simple. The situation presented itself as follows: I could take off my clothes, due to social pressure, and pretend to be at ease, or I could remain dressed and embrace my discomfort. Neither of these alternatives was appealing. What do you do in such awkward moments? You try to save time. I began removing my shirt, but very slowly, non-committally.

Social spaces cause restlessness because we want to be ourselves, and also part of a group. Theater director Amir Haddad told me that once, in a theater laboratory, he asked a group of people to undress. He then saw a young man who was completely naked but could barely hide his embarrassment. Amir went up to him and said that, if for him, being in his underwear was like being naked, that would be enough. Nudity is the extent to which each person can undress.

When the bus stopped in front of the beautiful sandy beach, all those naked Norwegians passed by me while I slowly removed my shoes, still counting on my socks as a last resort. The driver looked at me as if to define something important. Because I was the last one, I had no choice but to remove my pants and leave the bus, basking in the sun's warm embrace. Pretending to act naturally, I went to where people were leaving their belongings and threw myself into the sea. Holy transparency! That offered me some respite. No one had yet introduced themselves to me, but given the circumstances, I felt then compelled to do so.

The act of introducing ourselves to others is probably one of the moments that most resembles the act of getting dressed. We clothe ourselves with a desire to present ourselves to the world in a certain way. We want to have control over this process. This is the paradox of existing in the world while simultaneously embodying a character.

Thus, I began introducing myself to others, even though, in

my naked state, I struggled to recognize myself. We began conversing in the water, and I began to relax somewhat. The girls, who were all very pale, managed to overcome the water's tenuous translucency and, albeit slightly refracted, revealed themselves in detail before me. And the complete emancipation of nature evoked a strange sensation—a mix of distress and euphoria.

We all seemed pleased with that place and that moment in the sea. Between plunges into the salty water, we talked with each other and exchanged information, with me being the object of the most curiosity. They were all very friendly, but distant. I'm not certain about this, but I believe that Europeans tend to identify more with external nudity than with internal nudity. They expressed reservations that I wasn't sure were due to my interference with their group, or because they shared cultural similarities.

By the time someone shouted "Lunch!" I felt so at home that I imagined myself married to one of those girls and living in Oslo for the rest of my life. They were serving lunch on towels in the sand.

I couldn't believe it: the sea's protection had just calmed me down, and now I had to leave the water. Sitting naked and with naked people on the beach then presented a whole new challenge. In routine, trivial activities, nudity goes far beyond the issue of sexuality; it is a relationship with oneself and others that dates back to a very distant era. There was something primal and strange about sharing a meal with a group of naked people.

I know this is narrow-minded, but that's how I felt at the time, and now that I'm telling you, I see that day as a special time in my life. It was both a challenge and a learning experience to awaken to the shapes and nuances with which bodies reflect their surroundings. The world takes on previously unnoticed naked tones, and the silhouettes of the bodies add a new level of harmony to the landscape and surroundings.

Thank the good Lord, nights in the desert can be quite cold. As the evening approached, everyone got dressed again and I was able to return, so to speak, to the planet of clothes. And we continued our journey on the bus, with the goal of reaching Ras Muhammad, the extreme southernmost point of the Sinai, at the junction of the Gulf of Aqaba and the Red Sea. There was a lot of ground ahead, and given the late hour, we stopped in the middle of nowhere to have dinner and spend the night.

That trip required everyone to bring a sleeping bag, which I borrowed from an American friend. Americans tend to have extra equipment, and the latest novelties and gadgets in the world of consumption. My sleeping bag was of the chic-ist sort and filled me with confidence.

Back on that bus, where we returned to the world of clothing, people became more reticent. The intimacy I had experienced on the beach receded, and in its place, normal interaction between people who already knew each other and spoke the same language took over. I was a little upset that I couldn't continue what I thought were new and exotic friendships. I felt isolated again, looking out of the corner of my eye at the laughter and hearing conversations in Norwegian. Every now and then, I would participate with a smile, pretending to understand something that made me feel even more foreign.

Eventually, we chose a dune with a curious formation as our place to sleep for the night. The bus stopped in front of a mound of sand that stretched out like a wall for fifty or sixty meters. At the foot of this steep hill was placed our long line of sleeping bags. I got into my bag with the positive feeling that the next day would be better. That first-world sleeping bag provided me with a cozy feeling of protection. *Everything is going to be fine*, I thought, closing my eyes.

Suddenly, the wind started to blow. In the desert, wind does not mean air, but sand. The grains hit my sleeping bag's nylon with great force. Then they grew, popping more and more, giving way to a torrent of pops. I'd seen a lot of movie images of sandstorms in the desert, so I felt unfazed, and I simply pulled the zipper up to the top of the bag and fell asleep in my little Yankee Apache fort.

I woke up a few hours later, still in the middle of the night. And noticing that the sand grains had stopped popping, I opened the zipper a little to enjoy the fresh air and look at my surroundings. It was at that moment when I dread realized that the sleeping bags next to mine were all gone.

I opened the zipper and its clasp completely, and was horrified. There was no one there! There was no sleeping bag, no bus, and no connection to the world. I was alone in the Sinai desert. They had abandoned me in the middle of the desert!

A physical terror seized me. Do you know those moments of survival when you feel close to death? Well... looking one way, then the other, all the way down, all that I saw was an empty horizon. I looked every which way and the view was the same. Except for the moon and stars, there was no light.

What could have happened? I was thinking angrily. I can't believe those irresponsible people left me alone there. This is criminal.

I didn't want to believe it, but I thought that the sandstorm might have gotten worse, and I imagined what had happened: they'd run to the bus, where there was protection from the sandstorm, and they forgot all about me. Of course, there was no one to say, "What about Nilton?" So, not only did I feel abandoned in an inhospitable and uninhabited environment, but I also felt worthless. Not even you, driver?! You didn't even remember the embarrassed young man? Who was the prudish, judgmental companion you once shared glances and thoughts with?

I didn't know what to do. I contemplated remaining still, expecting that someone would suddenly realize that the person who at first hadn't been missed was now suddenly absent. The driver or the police would know how to recognize the place where we had spent the night. So I sat down, conformed like a condemned man, and stared at the merciless emptiness of the desert. Even celestial distances seemed more familiar and cozy than that place where I sat on the Earth. The desert sky is much more crowded than the ground, but on the ground all there is is the chilly reality of lifeless worlds, of planets deserted of presence. I thought, or rather despaired: *What should I do?*

I reassured myself, as if I were a child who needed to put on an oxygen mask before the plane crashed. What if I walk away? But where to? And if I do that, they will never be able to find me again. This rationality, however, is not simple. Inaction is revolting against the survival instinct. It feels unacceptable, akin to giving up. But I had to do something. I stood up several times, moved by this feeling, and controlled myself, arguing with myself and sitting down again. The longest hour of my life was passing, and there was no sign of anyone trying to rescue me.

What if they spent hours or days without remembering me? I couldn't accept that I was so insignificant. Human life matters, but your presence matters even more. Not having had enough influence to imprint my existence on that group was inhumane and shameful. I began to gently weep in despair; moments of helplessness and abandonment began to echo my emotions. Then I stood up one last time, now more panicked than resolved. I was going to start walking. I was going to choose a direction and follow it.

I walked a few meters when suddenly I heard inside my head, like a memory, someone asking, "What's on the other side?" Like a command from my dreams, or from the gods of the night. And slowly, as if a last ray of hope had dawned, I tiptoed beyond the long hill of dunes and saw on the other side a long row of sleeping bags, all lined up.

Someone had discovered during the night that sleeping on the other side of this natural wall would provide better shelter, and everybody but me had then followed. In the void, there are not only mirages of things that do not exist but also camouflages of those that do. The bus, in turn, had gone to a gas station a few dozen kilometers away to refuel so that we wouldn't waste time the next morning. The group was probably informed of this, but surely in Norwegian.

Forgotten alone on the other side of the dunes, and left without any information, seemed like a fitting metaphor for the nightmare of abandonment I had just been through. Without anyone to blame or complain to, I set up my sleeping bag and tried to fall asleep in the solitude of so many emotions, away from people and reality.

When I nestled my head into the nylon resting on the relative softness of the sand beneath, I realized the desperation that I could have given myself: if I had despaired and chosen a direction at random, I might have risked my life. Only then did I remember that whisper that, coming from the recesses of my memory, had asked me, "What's on the other side?" Indeed.

If the teacher and children were mere illusions, reality would have been even stranger. Certain things are more remarkable for their non-existence than for their existence. Perhaps this is how we hide our nudity: our clothes seem more real than our ghostly nakedness.

FATE AND THE FUTURE

My secretary opened the door and announced what was next. "The woman you allowed me to schedule—the one who was crying a lot and is not from the Jewish community—is here for her appointment."

I only vaguely remembered the situation. And before I could ask my secretary for details, a woman, approximately sixty years old, elegant, and with a tissue in her hand, entered my office. She sat down opposite me and, trying to compose herself, said: "Sorry, I'm very emotional, and I'm going through something very difficult... First of all, I would like to thank you for having me. Since I'm not Jewish, you're kind enough to give me your time."

Then she resumed her discreet crying, already looking for a new tissue in her bag. "You know, rabbi, I'm going to confess to you that I've already gone to several religious people from different traditions in search of an answer. I have several Jewish friends, and they told me a lot about you. So I took the liberty of asking for this meeting," she said, looking into my eyes.

Her preamble carried a distinct tone of defiance. In the past, during periods of increased religious intolerance, it was common to hold disputes to determine which religion or religious individual possessed the truth, as if some particular dogma could be the exclusive source of veracity. What had the other religious people said or suggested to her? I imagined that no one had been able to deal with the issue, whatever it was, and I imagined myself joining the list of failures.

"I respect all traditions, but no one can explain what happened to me. I'm coming here to see if you can give me an explanation."

We have now activated the red code, transitioning from the initial alert to a potential religious dispute. Explanation?! I'm unsure if the answers provided by religious traditions qualify as such.

From the Latin root *explicare*, the *ex* in explanation means "outside," "outwards," and *plicare* means "to fold." Explaining involves unfolding something so crumpled and twisted that it's difficult to understand. What may not fit well is the ex, i.e., the preposition that designates outside. Not everything in the spiritual world has to be external—a conception that often leads to fetishes that vulgarize the spiritual into "exspiritual."

"I will try to tell this long story as briefly as possible," she continued.

"I was very happily married; my life was a dream. My husband was wealthy, and we had a son. But everything started to go wrong when my second son was born. He was born with problems, and we couldn't take him home. He stayed in the hospital, and every day I went there to care for and pray for him. Then something unthinkable happened: my husband suddenly passed away."

Facing adversity like this, one after the other, is disorienting. The individual not only grapples with death and its attendant challenges but also experiences a disruption in their overall connection to life. For the human consciousness that contemplates future risks, it is crucial to maintain a sense of protection, a sense of having a future and a purpose, and a belief that certain events will not befall us. We hold these beliefs because we cannot guarantee that anything in the world, no matter how bizarre, will occur in our lives. It's scary.

"Rabbi, but that's nothing. For months, as a newly widowed person, I kept going to the hospital, trying to save that little life, but it wasn't possible. It was very hard, but I overcame it because there was no other choice. I had my other lovely son, and I needed to devote myself to him and take care of him."

She quickly wiped away tears that spilled down her face,

creating an increasingly awkward tone of gravity that caused me immense distress. The gestures and tone of her narrative hinted at a big question she was about to raise.

"He grew up handsome and intelligent. He multiplied and expanded the businesses he took over from his father, becoming a successful entrepreneur. A genius, and always very creative! I felt moved by this as if I were receiving a reward for those incredibly challenging years filled with longing and dashed dreams. Then, he was on the verge of getting married, complete with a grand celebration and a honeymoon at a ski resort—a sport he was passionate about. Everything was already purchased and contracted. Until, a few days before the wedding, he took a short trip, and that's when it all happened."

The crying gained strength. I waited for her to recover, saying nothing. Then she continued.

"It was a terrible accident, and he unexpectedly left us on the eve of the wedding, during a period of his life filled with immense joy. Do you understand? He was everything to me—everything! I didn't know how to live without him; I just don't know how to keep going."

Here it comes.

"The question I pose to you today tortures me—no one has provided a satisfactory answer..."

I was apprehensive. I was waiting for the big "Why?" or the hot spark of an indignant "How?!"

"I didn't come here to ask you why this all happened... I just want to know, '*How* could it have happened?'" she said, reading my thoughts.

The question, *How could it happen?* is a much more difficult one than *Why did it happen?* Human limitations and incapacity can justify the question of why by evoking hidden realities beyond our reach. On the other hand, the question of how suggests an uncovered reality that defies denial or repression. The event occurred, establishing it as a fact, objective, and impervious to neglect or dismissal.

How could it have happened? is an ancient book in the biblical canon that became known as Lamentations in the West. That woman was clearly in regret mode. She did not challenge me to face the feeble question of why, but rather, the reasonableness of all those circumstances. The answer of "I don't know, nobody knows," can always defeat why. Nevertheless, there is no checkmate or antidote to challenge *How?*

"How could it have happened, rabbi?"

I replied: "Was it your fault?"

"My fault?" she said, almost offended.

"I don't mean to suggest that you were the culprit, but your question seems to be ultimately one that only you can answer: How could it have happened?"

"I don't understand!" she said, perplexed, preparing to defend herself, and then regaining her composure with fresh indignation.

I continued: "How could you not have rebuilt your life? How could you have avoided getting married again and starting another family? How could you have put 'all your eggs in one basket'?"

She began to understand where I was pointing, but she was still filled with disbelief at hearing me speak so directly and coldly to a suffering and bitter person like herself.

"You are a lovely, intelligent woman. I'm talking about today, now, and I imagine you have always been so..." —I said, aware of the great risk I was taking.

"Me? How... Do you think so?" she replied, composing herself.

"The whole time you were telling me your story, I was wondering why you hadn't tried to rebuild your life. Were you young when all this happened? I mean, back then?"

"Yes, very young."

"So! 'How could this have happened?' It's because you had to place all your love bets in one direction. Of course, this does not explain, much less diminish, the regret and the mourning. However, it answers the question, *How?*"

I paused to see if she was following me.

"Do you think so?"

"Do I think what?"

"That I can rebuild my life? Could I, at my age, aspire to something?"

"Of course! You are an elegant, attractive, smart, and curious woman. Why wouldn't that be possible? This is particularly true for you, as you have encountered the 'impossible' numerous times in the most challenging circumstances. Why, then, do you not find it again in productive situations?"

"Do you think so?" she said, pensive. Her voice was already different as if it were someone else's. She was gazing into infinity as if my words were invigorating and renewing her.

"I came here to talk about the past, and you're making me think about the future," she considered, almost smiling.

And then, quoting her, I said: "You came here looking for an explanation, and you're going to leave with an implication!"

The center of life is not the ex of the external but rather the in of the internal. It was impossible to "unfold" such a situation without twisting it further. That meeting, and what that woman wanted, were about herself and her future. Human questions are always about the future, no matter how much the past has provoked them.

I can say that she left my office much lighter than she entered it. But I only know the story so far. I would never see her again after that day. It was fate that we met, but I don't believe her future was fated.

In our world, we associate mothers whose children leave before them, as an inversion of the natural order. It is natural (and maternal) to seek resources that help to maintain these severed bonds; such things can offer relief. However, it is critical to broaden our horizons toward life, which is finite and lies entirely ahead of us. Confronting and interrogating the how's of our lives does not yield many fruitful answers. But by inverting the how, and pointing it toward the future, rather than the past, then the how takes on the form of an answer, not a question.

We clamor to discover, despite everything, ways to continue living. And if we cannot control the reasons why bad things happen, then we are at least empowered to influence our future as best we are able.

The Angel of Death is said to have countless eyes (it's everywhere!). According to this perspective, when a dying person is about to die, the Angel of Death stands above the person's pillow, holding in his hands an unsheathed sword with a drop of gall hanging from the tip. When the sick person sees him, they tremble with fear and open their mouths in terror. At that moment, the angel makes a drop of bile fall inside the person's mouth, and they die. Their body then emits an odor, and their face turns green.

TALMUD, KET.77B

LIFE BEFORE DEATH

As a chaplain at the prestigious Memorial Sloan Kettering Hospital in New York City, I provided care for Jewish patients assigned to me across two floors of the building. I was finishing my studies, and my workload at the hospital was two days a week, carrying out the task of visiting these patients and offering them pastoral care.

I don't like the word "pastoral" because, in addition to being paternalistic, it seems to admit that those who are being helped are lambs, always prone to following someone.

There was a full-time rabbi who supervised me. The visits included practical help in the religious realm—providing religious materials such as books of Psalms, and facilitating more specific needs of patients, most importantly, talking with them and often offering religious comfort.

In Jewish tradition, visiting the sick is a common practice, but it is important to know how to do it in a way that meets the requirements of such delicate moments. Therefore, by "doing," we often mean not doing, and instead simply offering to be in the patient's sensitive emotional and spiritual space. The rabbi, the hospital's main chaplain, and a professional psychologist, each with their unique skills, were both there to supervise us to ensure that this was done well.

The psychological counselor requested that we transcribe some of the conversations verbatim for analysis purposes. In the zigzag pattern of lines in a dialogue, we can discern a significant amount of information. We can see that the patient, often reluctant to open up, at a given moment offers access.

These transcriptions revealed something else tellingly, as well. It became clear to us that it's not uncommon for the person carrying out the visit to divert the conversation to something milder, less serious, rather than accept the invitation to delve deeply into a person's emotional depths. This usually happens unconsciously, rather than intentionally. The advisor highlighted and exposed these moments, and I was surprised to see myself practicing this sort of evasion.

The first mistake I made, happened right there with the patient, when he offered an opening, an opportunity for us to enter an area of intimacy, and I subtly rejected it, proposing some disconnected or irrelevant subject instead. The second error happened during the transcription of the conversations themselves, when I failed to recognize the emotions captured in those poignant paragraphs. In other words, I evaded what mattered most not once but twice.

It was a skill that I was trying to gain, but it wasn't simple, since sometimes patients look like our parents, our grandparents, our friends, and—the worst of all worlds—like ourselves. For reasons of insecurity or direct identification, the rabbi/chaplain/trainee shifts their focus away from the patient they are visiting, subconsciously desiring some other outcome.

I tried to improve and meet the challenges. However, during the learning process, challenges often become more difficult. Once, while doing rounds on my floor, I saw a new patient on my list. I found it strange that the title Rabbi came before his first name. When I opened the door, I came across something alarming: lying on the bed, there was an Orthodox rabbi with a long beard, surrounded by his disciples wearing traditional black suits. The patient was a rebbe, a wise rabbi of notable position, who led a Hasidic group in Brooklyn and was undergoing palliative treatment.

When his disciples saw me, the look of astonishment and rejection was immediate. On seeing my skullcap and my beardless face, they understood everything they needed: first, that I was a chaplain; second, that I did not follow the Orthodox movement's understandings of Jewish teaching and practice. Still, I mustered courage, went to the rabbi, and introduced myself.

His followers' energy made me feel like talking to him was heresy. Still, we chatted a bit, and he was pleasant. He answered some questions while I was looking for ways out of the situation, both to avoid being invasive and to escape the moments of silence, during which I could hear the silently shouted question, *What is this man doing here?!*

I felt a sense of relief as I departed. I had felt affronted, and was insecure. Really, what could I do there, surrounded by rabbis with more mileage than myself? He, a nonagenarian, is a mentor to all those others; what could he hear from me? What help could I provide him with? Talk about life? Or death? Was there anything I knew that he didn't, either through experience or the knowledge I possessed at the time?

But the rebbe was on my floor, so all of my rounds included visiting his room. The next day, I tried to be helpful, offering to solve a serious problem: his wife was staying in an apartment hotel opposite the hospital so that she could visit him and assist him daily. But on Saturday, there was a problem: the hospital doors were automatic, and observing the Sabbath prohibited you from using electricity, even indirectly. She was standing in front of the hospital unable to enter because opening the door would have violated Shabbat. I arranged for a side door to remain open all day on Saturday—it was even the middle of winter!—so that she could visit without any problems.

Subsequently, I assisted in resolving an issue with the rebbe's kosher food; his radical stance led him to reject the rabbinic supervision seal on the hospital's kosher meals. I stepped in to facilitate the procurement of food from an alternate supplier. So I was endeavoring to fulfill my duties effectively. However, having to go into that room, pull up a chair, and talk to the rebbe terrified me!

What could I impart to him that he wasn't already aware of from his insightful life, and what could spare me from being ridiculed for my inexperience and naivete? I was unsure if he would accept my qualifications; likely, he wouldn't, and there's a chance that he might even offend or insult me. I found it all very intimidating. I admit that the issue wasn't so much about him personally, but rather the constant presence and critical gaze of his disciples, which made me feel like an imposter, a charlatan masquerading as someone I wasn't. Difficult energy!

Using my cunning, a resource we turn to when we are in trouble or a squeeze, I started visiting him when he was asleep. I would pass by the door, and when I saw that he was dozing, I would enter and leave a card that read, "Your chaplain was here while you were asleep and wishes you a speedy recovery. Signed..."

Although this card was a useful tool, it required careful use. Shortly thereafter, the main chaplain questioned me, stating that he had visited the rabbi on my floor and observed a pile of those cards on the table. After acknowledging my difficulties, he advised me to persist without feeling embarrassed. He emphasized that this gentleman was facing a problem and that I should continue to offer my services until he requested a suspension of the visits. He reiterated that he didn't expect me to respond brilliantly to the man's challenges and that my mere presence was already of immense value. I told him I would try.

I did try, I think, without much success because the visits were brief and did not progress beyond meager sentences, both in form and content.

But one day, as I was doing my rounds, I saw through the half-open door that an emergency team was helping the rebbe. The atmosphere exuded an indelible terror—one that arises when life and death collide. I believe it was due to the role I played, but perhaps it was also because of the bond I had already formed with my patient, which made me feel closer.

When I arrived at the bedroom door, one of the disciples was standing just outside. He lifted the badge from my lapel, read it silently and disdainfully, then made a dismissive sign and whispered something in Yiddish like, "It's not necessary." I accepted my dismissal and turned around.

But as I walked away, I heard a commotion and, turning back, I saw in the distance that the emergency team was finishing its procedures. In turn, the calmer movement and relaxed expressions appeared to be clear signs of the problem's resolution. Then, among the nurses and doctors, I noticed the rebbe, who had removed his oxygen mask, waving in my direction. With slow steps, I approached the room again. This time, another adept who was near him came towards me and said, "The rebbe wishes to speak to you."

I went with this man to the threshold of the rebbe's room. "He has requested to be alone with you," the man added, appearing somewhat perplexed by the request and conveying a sense of strangeness. As a result of this I wanted to confirm the information: "Does he want to be alone with me?"

He glanced at me, shrugged in confirmation, and appeared just as surprised as I was. Then he left and closed the door, leaving me alone in the room with the rebbe in his bed. Never before had I been alone with him.

I tried to compose myself, and with an air of naturalness, sat down beside him. He looked at me candidly. I gestured to hold his hand, and he consented. I remained silent for a few moments, hand-in-hand with him, resisting my urge to say something, not wanting to compromise the mystery of that moment and the way things would unfold.

Looking deep into my eyes, the rebbe asked me in English, "What do you think will happen to me?"

His voice was serene, as if he came from another world. He had been cordial in using English to communicate. Adherents of

Orthodox Judaism, as practiced in Hasidic circles, usually speak Yiddish. I could barely speak Yiddish, and his use of English felt like an act of intimacy.

Like a riddle, the question echoed through the room and into my heart. I tried a classic apprentice move and took a risk: "What do you think will happen to you?" For a tenth of a second, it seemed to me that this movement gave some legitimacy to the fact that I was there alone with him, holding his hand.

Then, even more quietly than the first time, he shook his head negatively and said, "No. What do you think will happen to me?" And by stressing the "you," he left me no room to maneuver.

I took a deep breath, breathing in my soul and looking into his eyes, and said, "I think you are going to die."

My sentence's finiteness was absolute, and it hung dry between us. He joined his other hand to the one I was already holding and, squeezing it, began to repeat serenely, "Thank you. Thank you. Thank you." He kept repeating this for a long time. The repetition was an explicit attempt to highlight what would come at the end. Then he concluded, "Thank you for saying goodbye. Thank you for saying goodbye to me."

An emotional charge compressed both of our larynxes. The lump in the throat, which typically occurs when we contract our muscles to contain tears, was visible. However, I believe it wasn't so much about containing the tears, but rather about experiencing their solid and tough taste. His hands tightened more than before, and there was a new silence. This one, however, no longer bothered me; I felt part of it, producing it in unison.

Again, he spoke: "Can you say the *Vidui* to me?"

Jews recite the Vidui prayer at the end of life as a form of extreme unction. The dying person must recite this prayer, which translates to "Confession." Only in cases when the person no longer has the conscious means of doing so should another individual say it to the dying person. He was there, telling me to represent him!

Now, what comes next in this story is a true horror. Putting my hand in my pocket, I realized I hadn't brought the small book containing the essential prayers for use in a hospital setting. And I didn't know it by heart! Yes, I knew some parts of it, but as a true beginner, with the excitement and nervousness of the moment, I feared I wouldn't be able to remember anything! And it was clear that there was no need to hesitate, but rather to move forward in the adventure of the relationship that was already underway.

So I started stitching together the fragments of the Vidui Hebrew text. In some parts, he quietly corrected me, as if he were covering the gaps I didn't know. He performed with such mastery and delicacy that I never lost control of the act. I was like a friend holding hands, helping him cross a river, stone by stone. I asked for his name in Hebrew, and he requested that I personalize the prayer.

In the end, there was a peace that was not of this world. I was holding hands with him; I felt the warmth of his presence and a soft cold sensation, as if my hands could enter a little territory that at that moment was not mine. We stayed together, teary-eyed and surrounded by a silence that only eternal friends can share. Then he fell asleep.

I left the room in a total state of contemplation, as if I had participated in a miracle or something outside of reality. When the disciple saw me outside the room, he partially awakened me, curiously running towards me, asking, "What was it? What did he tell you?"

He questioned me as if I owed him something. And I spontaneously made—I swear it wasn't any kind of revenge—a gesture similar to the shrug he had given me when he looked at my badge and showed his disdain. It was as if he were transparent and didn't exist—as if his curiosity simply didn't exist. And I continued on without reply.

I returned home, trying to decode what had happened. I'd experienced something profound and instructive for life. It is clear that the rebbe, an experienced and sensitive person, had noticed my ambiguous feelings and embarrassment during previous visits. And at that moment when he was very close to the procedures and the final moments of his life, he made a vital and essential movement. Life only ends when it ends. Until our last breath, we have a clear mandate over our existence.

He was surrounded by supporters, all of whom probably used vulgar clichés such as "Everything will be fine," "You will soon be cured," and the like. But his isolation was more profound than mere loneliness, as his supporters actively anticipated his death by neglecting to be there with him at the crucial moment. And I, who in my naïve presence managed to join eyes and souls with him, had been there, together and present, breaking his solitude.

This is how I pieced together the details of this incident. The rebbe, surrounded by unresponsive attendants, looked around and, in the distance, saw the young almost-rabbi. This was his chance. He brought me closer, and this enabled a moment of full life, which is always where people meet. And where do they meet? In the place where they are truly together, forming a complete connection.

He needed a Vidui—a whole moment that would allow him to be where he really was and not run away. He saw in me the chance to do this, and the only way to do it is together: me for him and him for me. I broke his hypocrisy of loneliness, and he ordained me a rabbi, empowering me by legitimizing my ability and making me the chosen one to be there at that moment. Becoming aware of that power precisely when he was in the place of greatest possible impotence—devoid of a future, tied to a bed, and ripped from the soil that had nourished him for almost a century of life—was something that untangled many knots and bonds.

I will never forget those moments—moments that everyone would consider "without quality," yet they resonate to this day with the power of a piece of eternity. I fantasize that my hands holding his entered that tunnel at the end of life and that something eternal about him also remained ingrained in my skin and my soul, here on this side.

Two days later, when I started my shift, I hurried to the rebbe's room. The place appeared to be a newly sanitized hospital room, waiting for a new guest and a new destination. He had passed away the day before. I then realized that I didn't even know his name! I want to cherish and honor his name forever. After all, my formal ordination would take place in just three weeks, as scheduled. Even though the rebbe had already approved it and made it real.

So I hurried to the central ward, which housed the nursing department and contained clipboards and folders with patient information. Since this central character in my life had been anonymous and only known by his title, I wanted to know his real name. My junior chaplain status, however, prevented me from obtaining information about patients who had already undergone "discharge."

To this day I know nothing about the identity of the rebbe, his life story, and the community he served. He thus became a mythical character, one of those from legendary tales like "Once upon a time there was a king or a queen..."—whose identity dispenses further description.

Many people imagine a tunnel connecting this world with the afterlife. There are reports of individuals who have been extradited, either due to pending issues or by divine grace. In my case, something opposite seemed to have happened: it was as if I had been at the frontier of frontiers, saying goodbye, perhaps with my hands already in the external field of this world—reflections of the bluish celestial light upon them. I had also seen someone prove that life exists before death, that full existence is possible until the end, and that we have presence and autonomy until this moment.

For the disbelievers, here is my testimony: Yes, there is life right before death, on the brink of death!

THE SPIRIT OF IPANEMA

It wasn't long after the episode with the rebbe that another situation occurred at Memorial Sloan Kettering Hospital. In fact, this happened just one week later.

During the time I worked there, the AIDS virus emerged. It was terrible because Memorial Sloan Kettering was the main state-of-the-art hospital in Manhattan, and many of the infected patients went there. Initially, most of the AIDS patients were from the gay community, and many of them were Jews. Jews have an inexplicable mathematical peculiarity: they are a minority that, regardless of the group we direct our attention to—activists, artists, scientists, traders, doctors, or thinkers—seems to be much greater than their actual number. The task of caring for several Jews who had contracted HIV was a powerful experience in my life.

A lack of information and the fear of contracting the disease were enormous. We visited patients dressed as astronauts—something familiar to the COVID-19 pandemic, but not at all common at the time. I was already finishing my studies and would soon return to Brazil. The terror of AIDS, added to the anxiety of health professionals generally, made me want to end my activities as a chaplain, a position that had been deeply important to me.

One day, I saw a new patient on my list. He was a young man, but I found out that this was not a case of AIDS. Rarely did you find young people in experimental hospitals or on "medical floors"—the term for those that housed the most hopeless clinical cases and studies of new drug treatments. The majority of people on the medical floors were older. There were young people, too, but thank

God they were a small minority. And seeing a patient in their twenties without AIDS was rare.

I entered the room and saw a young man in pajamas with his legs crossed on the bed covers watching television. At first, engrossed in a program, he didn't take his eyes off the TV. I offered my two or three ready-made sentences, asking who he was and what he was doing there. He seemed uninterested, giving me no more than a few glances so as not to be completely rude, or make me feel entirely irrelevant.

"Chaplain? Oh... okay. Thanks, maybe another time." He spoke without losing focus on the TV. I noticed his eyes were green, and I knew that green eyes were caused by the sclera, not the iris or pupil.

I saw that his name was Paul. He was coming off some rounds of chemotherapy and seemed to be in entirely his own world. He was a good-looking young man. I was curious to learn about his case, but I didn't receive much of a welcome.

"No problem," I said. "I'll come by another time to see if you want to talk."

"Okay," he stated quite firmly, and I started to make my exit.

"What accent is that?" he suddenly interjected into the silence, seeming to notice me for the first time.

I replied, "Portuguese."

"Portuguese? Um... from Brazil? I know someone from Brazil; maybe you know them."

I understood this was a counter-order, and I moved towards his bed. "Brazil is big!" I replied with a smile, expecting some kind of American-style joke in which Brazil would have Buenos Aires as its capital and its inhabitants would all live in small villages by the sea.

"She's from Rio de Janeiro... You're from Rio?"

Before I could respond, he added: "And by the way, my name is Paul. Sorry, I didn't introduce myself."

“I’m from Rio!” I offered.

“This person I spoke about is a beautiful woman. I fell madly in love with her. And you, are you a rabbi? Are you going to be a rabbi in Brazil?”

“Yes, in two weeks I will receive my rabbinic ordination.”

“Beautiful. She is beautiful. I was totally in love. I went to a nightclub with a group, and there were Brazilians present. I danced with her right away. They even played lambada! Do you like lambada?” He asked this with the drawl of a foreigner who enjoys chewing on unfamiliar words as if they were from a Carmen Miranda film.

“Was she from Rio?” I asked.

“Yes, she was from Rio, and she was Jewish.” He began to laugh to himself as if he were imagining an untested coincidence.

“Her name was Rafaela Zilberstein? Do you know her?”

I stopped.

“Are you kidding me? That’s the name of my older brother’s girlfriend, who lives in Rio... I don’t believe there are two of them.”

A slight embarrassment set in, but he undid it as if it were nothing.

“This is crazy! I met your brother’s girlfriend and fell in love with her!” he said with a smile, and his greenish eyes looking into infinity.

“But nothing happened. She did not even acknowledge my presence. She only danced with me once. The group was so joyful.” This was the era of discotheques and famous nightclubs in New York, which would also make their way into Rio’s nightlife. “This is amazing. What are the chances of this happening?” he concluded, falsely impressed.

At that moment, a very lovely young woman entered the room. It was his sister, a blonde woman with the figure and appearance of a model. Paul was also very handsome, movie heartthrob style.

I would later discover that his mother had been a model and that she'd brought many of New York's famous figures to their knees.

"Susan, this is... I forgot to ask for your name."

"Nilton."

"This is Rabbi Nilton... In just three weeks, he will become Rabbi Nilton. You will be astounded to learn that it is his brother's girlfriend who I fell in love with—the woman I previously mentioned to you."

Susan looked at me and tried to put the pieces of that puzzle together.

I realized that this flirtation with my brother's girlfriend—look, what a crazy coincidence!—was a topic that excited Paul. His sister Susan was happy to see her brother in a good mood because of my presence there. It's always nice when you please a pretty woman, even if it's because of things unrelated to her.

An intriguing link was formed. Tropical Brazil, seductive Rio, and that passionate night remained in Paul's memory. All of that stripped me of the habit of a boring rabbi who would talk about life and death, ask about the past, and exaggerate positive expectations regarding the future. Everything had acquired a new context, full of light and warmth, tropical adventures, and youthfulness.

On my visits to the hospital over the next weeks, Paul and I spent fun times together. We kept talking nonsense, and, to try to boost his morale, I started to feed his imagination about Rio and Brazil: toucans, green and yellow, girls, beaches, and so many wonderful things from the virile land of South America. I just needed to change the skullcap for one of those exaggerated hats made of bananas and pineapples that recur in the Carmen Miranda Hollywood film version of Brazil. The truth is that it made him cheerful, and he always asked me when I would be back. We held numerous meetings to reminisce about Brazil as I was on the verge of completing my studies and returning to Rio de Janeiro.

I remember my last trip to the hospital. Paul was about to start a new round of chemotherapy, and there were doubts about whether he would survive the poison. However, we joked that he would heal and take a sabbatical to go and experience the imaginary carnival in Brazil that we had worked on in the last few weeks. I'd devised a fictitious activity that centered around healing, conquering all obstacles, and witnessing his vibrant youth resume his life's interrupted festivities. Paul was a successful Wall Street lawyer, but after all this, what he wanted most was to celebrate life. Brazil was the place, and if his health passed through customs, he'd be there soon.

My heart was moved that day. I imagined this would be the final time I'd see Paul. We said goodbye, and soon after, I returned to Brazil as a rabbi.

* * *

For whatever reason, we know people with whom a spirit-to-spirit interaction has been established. The spirit is a pattern—a fitting design. "Spirit" is the right word, even for beliefs that deal with the continuity of presences after death. "Soul," for example, is a kind of essence, something that somehow inflates our being. It animates and gives substance to what is flesh and blood. But the spirit is a matrix, a mold of our embodiment. Spirit contains our characteristics, a kind of alter-personality that, even without a body, still represents us. This non-corporeal identity, whether real or imaginary, is the nature of spirit. And wherever there is a person's specific smell, appearance, touch, and pattern, there is their spirit.

* * *

I once went to the city of York, England with my wife. It was a Friday and I wanted to go to a religious service in a synagogue.

There weren't any in the city. I would have to travel some twenty miles to Leeds. So I resigned myself to not going, and, as we had nothing else to do, I managed to sign us up at the last minute for a ghost tour of the city of York.

I knew this was all part of a package tour to explore the old legends of haunted castles in the area. I thought it would be simple and perhaps old-fashioned, like an amusement park. It was actually like that, at first, until the night began to fall. Then the guide told us to sit on some steps leading up to a platform. I turned to my wife and whispered that the Sabbath was starting and that I would rather be in synagogue than listening to nonsense about ghosts. I'd barely finished saying this when the guide said, "Do you know where you are? You are on the steps of the old synagogue, of what was once the York synagogue."

The Clifford Tower fire, a twelfth-century event, had brutally killed the Jews of York. They were trapped, burned alive with their families, and would become spirits that haunted the city. Yet, York was never again able to erase these individuals from its identity. Their presence still resonates, and they are more significant than so many others who departed and left no trace—at least not in this way, so entangled with the city. Their spirits marked that place, leaving a type of shadow that still haunts York today.

* * *

Having left New York, returned to Brazil, and spent my first year as a rabbi in Rio de Janeiro, one fine day the phone rang and my secretary told me it was a call from abroad.

"Nilton?"

I couldn't identify the voice at first, but it continued: "This is Paul, from Memorial Sloan Kettering!"

It was like listening to a spirit, but of course I remembered Paul! I had just placed him in the lost people sector, either because of my move to Brazil or because of the conditions in which I'd seen him the last time we were together. He was resurfacing in my memory—a pattern, a spirit.

"Nilton? Can you hear me?" I must have been communicating my surprise with silence. Paul kept going: "I'm cured! Completely cured! And you know what else? I'm going to Brazil. I will follow your advice and experience the most exceptional year of my life. Realize a dream!"

I felt completely paralyzed at first. Rio de Janeiro was going through a terrible period. The economy was terrible. There were robberies everywhere, and a new wave of kidnappings had just begun. There was only talk of fear and social chaos. I pondered, *My God, how is this guy going to adjust to the environment down here?* Who could guarantee anything similar to the fantasies that I consistently used to motivate him? How could I take responsibility for those technicolor dreams in light of the gray reality that the city was going through?

He noticed my silence again on the line. I realized I needed to say something. "Paul! I'm thrilled for you! Rio? Are you really coming down here?"

"Not only am I coming to Rio, but just like we dreamed, I'm coming to Rio for a whole year! I need your help locating an apartment. I intend to become a *Carioca*." (That's what we call a native of Rio.)

I hung up the phone in a panic. I was a young rabbi working very hard, under constant scrutiny. How could I keep up with the pace and expectations of those impossible hospital dreams? What most frightened me was the prospect of causing Paul significant disappointment, as I had exaggerated and portrayed his fantasy in vivid detail. There would be no way for reality to match the fiction of what we'd imagined together.

I got a friend's apartment to rent for Paul. He came and made his dream come true, detail by detail. He learned Portuguese quickly and started speaking like a native. I don't know how, but he also became an expert in lambada and followed Rio's nightlife as if he were a local. Everyone knew him at clubs, restaurants, and everywhere. He was the man! I accompanied him to various locations where the waiters bowed respectfully. Everyone adored him, and the most renowned individuals in Ipanema held him in high regard. He became the very spirit of the place, and it was so magical that I couldn't believe it.

Everything unfolded exactly as envisioned as if the fantasy had acquired unrestricted rights and special permission to materialize. I was impressed by the way the "stars" aligned, how a plan that began with a coincidence ultimately connected our destinies. We became best friends and brothers, a bond that continues to this day.

Paul became a legend in the Ipanema neighborhood. He was, in fact, more of an enlightened figure than a haunting spirit. He, who would have become a mere memory, had materialized into a central character in my life and the lives of many others around me. From his green eyes to the gray of the disease, Paul had repainted the entire scene. His spirit prevailed, and his body had to follow his imagination. What a credit to Rio that, in contrast to York, it's a blessed and joyfully haunted city!

ABOUT THE AUTHOR

Nilton Bonder was trained and ordained at The Jewish Theological Seminary in New York City. He lectures regularly in the United States. Born in Brazil, he's a best-selling author of twenty-nine books in Latin America, leads one of Brazil's most influential Jewish congregations, and is active in civil rights and ecological causes. Some of his books have been translated in Europe and Asia and twelve of them in the U.S., including *The Kabbalah of Money* and *The Kabbalah of Food*, published by Shambhala. He's led workshops for corporations such as IBM and Globo Network Television, and delivered lectures at Boston University, New York Central Library, American Academy of Psychoanalysis, The Open Center, and Omega Institute. He lives in Rio de Janeiro and New York City.

OTHER NEW JEWISH BOOKS FROM MONKFISH

LIVING IN THE PRESENCE: A PERSONAL QUEST FOR THE BAAL SHEM TOV **RABBI BURT JACOBSON**

A rabbi's lifelong journey to discover the source and inspiration of Hasidism.

"Burt has striven his entire life to hand over the legacy of Hasidism and of my father to generations to come. Let us listen to his voice in the pages of this book so that we may be enriched by our Hasidic inheritance and offer that heritage as a great fire of passionate devotion to God, to one another, to our fragile earth to generations to come." —**Susannah Heschel**

ZEN MIND, JEWISH MIND: KOAN, MIDRASH, AND THE LIVING WORD **RAMI SHAPIRO**

The questioning perennial beginner is central to both Zen and Jewish. Rabbi Rami demonstrates a daring, iconoclastic, often humorous mind devoted to shattering the words, texts, isms, and ideologies on which expert mind—closed to inquiry—depends.

"A great way to deepen your spiritual life is to take a deep dive into a tradition other than your own—especially if you have a competent guide, and Rabbi Rami is an extraordinary guide. Not into Zen? Not a Jew? Not a problem. Anyone on any path will benefit enormously from this profoundly illuminating book." —**Philip Goldberg**, author of *American Veda*

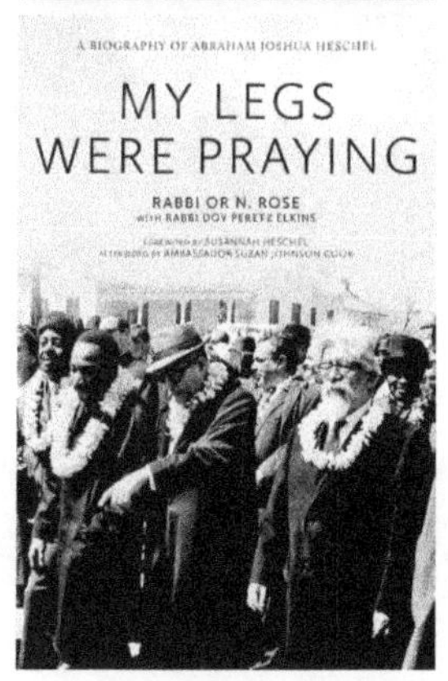

MY LEGS WERE PRAYING: A BIOGRAPHY OF ABRAHAM JOSHUA HESCHEL **RABBI OR N. ROSE**

Succinct, inspiring biography of a bridge-building Jewish leader, supplemented by 16 black-and-white photographs

"Amazing! I know a lot about Heschel, but this book is so full of detail about his life and clarity about his beliefs, I learned more." —**Ruth Messinger**, global ambassador, American Jewish World Service

"In this beautiful new biography, Rose brings Rabbi Abraham Joshua Heschel's story, indeed his inner light, to life for a new generation." —**Eboo Patel**, founder and president, Interfaith America

AVAILABLE FROM BOOKSELLERS EVERYWHERE

MONKFISH BOOK PUBLISHING • RHINEBECK, NEW YORK • MONKFISHPUBLISHING.COM

www.ingramcontent.com/pod-product-compliance
Lightning Source LLC
Jackson TN
JSHW020226230225
79529JS00001B/2

* 9 7 8 1 9 5 8 9 7 2 6 8 7 *